# OVER
# the
# EDGE

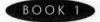

## <sup>A</sup> Chloe & Levesque
### MYSTERY

**BOOK 1**

Norah McClintock

The Chloe and Levesque Series

**Over the Edge**
**Double Cross**

# OVER the EDGE

A Chloe & Levesque

MYSTERY

BOOK 1

Norah McClintock

A DIVISION OF EDC PUBLISHING

First American Edition 2010
Kane Miller, A Division of EDC Publishing

Over the Edge. Copyright © 2000 by Norah McClintock.
All rights reserved. First published by Scholastic Canada Ltd.

All rights reserved.
For information contact:
Kane Miller, A Division of EDC Publishing
PO Box 470663
Tulsa, OK 74147-0663
www.kanemiller.com
www.edcpub.com

Library of Congress Control Number: 2009942492

Printed and bound in the United States of America
1 2 3 4 5 6 7 8 9 10
ISBN: 978-1-935279-67-9

*To Bruce and Bruce and Marlene*
*— who were a little odd in high school*

# Chapter 1

Peter Flosnick wasn't the kind of guy you'd expect to just vanish. I don't know why, but I always figured guys like him liked their lives. Sure, they were outside of things, but they were outside because they were obsessed with, well, whatever they were obsessed with. For some of them, it was computers. For others, mechanical stuff, engines or electronics. For Peter Flosnick it was the stars, as in twinkle, twinkle. He watched them. He studied them. He did science projects about them — award-winning science projects. And he wrote about them in the school newspaper, in an amateur astronomy column that appeared in three different local papers, and in a star-watching column in a kids' magazine. Whenever I saw him around school, he either had his nose in a book — studying up on the history, trajectory or probable life cycle of yet another heavenly body — or in one of those science magazines that are the official badge of nerd-dom. I used to see him around town, too, wandering up a trail in the park or down by the lake, speaking into a pocket-sized tape recorder. I figured, the guy's strange. I also figured he liked it that way — he'd probably keep on being strange until the day he died.

How I found out about Peter's disappearance is this: I had just dragged myself out of bed — not exactly my favorite activity, I might add. From the top of the stairs I smelled fresh-brewed coffee, bacon and toast. It was the coffee that interested me. I'm a mess without my morning fix of caffeine. When I got there, Phoebe — my younger sister — was sitting at the table, shoving a crust of toast into her mouth. She washed it down with the dregs of a glass of orange juice, then leapt up and dropped a kiss onto Levesque's cheek. He was standing at the stove, frying bacon.

A word about Levesque. Louis Levesque. Mom keeps telling us we should call him Dad, which Phoebe, Little Miss Tell-Me-What-You-Want-and-I'll-Be-Only-Too-Glad-to-Do-It, does. At least Levesque doesn't push the issue. He says I can call him Louis, which I do sometimes. But in my head I always think of him the way he was referred to in the newspapers back home: just plain Levesque. Mom married him a year ago. Two months ago he took a job in East Hastings, and here we are. Some of us — well, me — are not thrilled with his career move. Phoebe loves it here. So does Mom. My older sister, Brynn, escaped exile by graduating from high school. She's in college back in Montreal.

Levesque watched Phoebe race out the door to volleyball practice. An amused smile, barely visible below his bristling moustache, softened his large, square face. For a moment he looked like a regular dad on a regular weekday morning, instead of Mr. Officer-of-the-Law, cop-on-duty, the guy with the quickest, sharpest eyes in town. *Look smart, there, pal, I know who you are and I saw what you did.* Then the front door slammed shut and Levesque turned his attention to me.

"Juice?" he said. His tone was pleasant enough, but his eyes were burning into me, as if he were looking for something. He always seemed to be looking for something. I hadn't gotten used to that yet. That look of his always made me feel guilty, even when I hadn't done anything wrong.

"Just coffee, thanks," I said. I hooked the coffee pot off its warmer pad before he could do it for me.

"Eggs?" he said.

"No, thanks."

"Bacon? Toast?"

"No, thanks," I said again.

"You should reconsider. You know what they say, breakfast is the most important meal of the day."

I dribbled a little milk into my coffee and thought of plenty of things to say, starting with, hey, Sherlock, have you ever, in the whole year you've known me, seen me eat anything even remotely resembling breakfast? But Levesque could be a pit bull. If I started trying to be smart with him, I could be there all morning. He'd never let go. And besides breakfast, an argument was my least favorite start to the day.

I drank my coffee standing at the sink, looking out the window so that I could make a quick getaway if he decided to keep pestering me with questions. He didn't — he didn't have time to because the phone rang. Levesque handed me the

3

fork, said, "Watch that for me, will you?" and padded across the kitchen floor in sock feet to answer it.

I prodded the sizzling bacon. I would never have admitted it to Levesque, but it sure smelled good. I wondered whether he would notice if I sneaked a piece out of the pan. Probably, I decided. The guy was a detective, after all. Still, my mouth watered, and no matter how hard I tried I couldn't stop thinking how great it would taste to bite down on a strip of crisp, salty bacon.

"Did you talk to his mother?" Levesque was saying into the phone. "Did she have any ideas?" His eyes narrowed and his mouth twisted down, giving his face a look of concentration that I recognized all too well. His cop expression. Whoever he was talking to was talking business. "Okay," Levesque said. "Okay, I'll be right there."

He hung up the phone and disappeared from the kitchen. He was back a moment later with his jacket over his arm and his shoes in his hand.

"You know a kid named Flosnick?" he asked as he tied his laces.

"Peter Flosnick?" It sounds terrible now, under the circumstances, but I remember thinking, what could a mega-nerd like Peter Flosnick possibly have done to get himself in trouble with the police? "I know who he is. Why?"

"He's missing."

"Missing?"

"His mother hasn't seen him since Sunday

evening."

This was Tuesday morning.

"Apparently he wasn't at school yesterday, either. You have any ideas?"

"Me?" He had to be kidding. Okay, so I wasn't the big-league joiner Phoebe had turned into — she had signed up for the swim team and the volleyball team, after one debate she had turned into the star of the junior debating team, she had already been elected assistant editor of the yearbook and treasurer of the student council, and for the first time in her life she had zillions of friends. I, on the other hand, was taking a little longer to get my bearings. But that didn't mean I was desperate enough to have a fix on Peter Flosnick's comings and goings. It was just that my friends were back in Montreal, not here.

"I said I know who he *is*," I told Levesque. "But that doesn't mean I know anything about him."

Levesque's moustache twitched, a sure sign he was smiling somewhere under it. "Not your type?" he asked. When I didn't answer he said, "A lot of police work is about asking questions. Sometimes you get lucky and get some answers you can use." He got up and slipped into his jacket.

"What about your breakfast?" I asked.

"No time."

I turned the heat off under the pan, lifted out the bacon strips and set them on a piece of paper towel to drain. The front door clicked shut. I looked at the bacon and took another sip of my coffee. Then I

5

began to eat the bacon one piece at a time.

Thirty minutes later, I was thinking and feeling and wishing the same thing I had thought and felt and wished every weekday morning for the past six weeks.

Look, this is me, standing face-to-face with the enemy and thinking: shoot me now and put me out of my misery. But, of course, that had already happened. I *had* been shot. Or run over or drowned or dropped off a cliff or fired out of a cannon. I was living in East Hastings, wasn't I, a big pit of nickel and boredom. The bottom line was the same: I had died and now here I was in a town called . . . Well, never mind. I was doomed to tread the same path each and every morning, doomed to end up where I was right now, staring down the enemy. Staring it down and being swallowed up by it all at the same time. There was no escape.

Now this is me looking down at my feet. Looking down at my sneakers and wishing they were ruby slippers. This is me wishing I believed in magic and fairy tales and good witches, wishing I could click my heels together and find myself back home in my own version of Kansas — which for me is Montreal. Okay, so technically Montreal wasn't my home anymore, but it still felt more like home than East Hastings ever would.

Now this is me raising my head and wishing I would see the big cross that stands on the top of Mount Royal in the middle of Montreal. I used to be able to see it from the front of my old school.

This is me raising my head and actually seeing East Hastings Regional High, built in the style of the nineteen sixties, with a ratio of brick to windows of about a thousand to one. The school as bunker, designed to keep distractions out, window cleaning bills to a minimum and window repair bills lower still. Twelve hundred kids trudge to and from East Hastings Regional every day. Twelve hundred kids who have no idea what they're missing, stuck up here in a cluster of dots on a map, a handful of little towns that no one in Toronto or Montreal or Vancouver has ever heard of, or, if they have, they can never place. "Where exactly is that?" my friends asked me when I told them where I was going. It's right here, compadres. It's this rinky-dink town where everyone speaks the same language, *ici on ne parle pas français,* where there's no rue St-Denis, no Place d'Armes, no Carré St-Louis, no Gare Centrale, no boulevard René-Levesque, no mountain you can climb to the top of and look out on a sea of twinkling lights. No St. Lawrence River, no Laurentian autoroute, no school trips to ski Mont Tremblant.

And — did I mention this? — there's no escape. Not in the short term. Not that I've discovered. So, here we go, you place one foot in front of the other and repeat as often a necessary until you reach the top of the steps and — whoa! — look at that pair sitting on the wall. How sweet. Just what we all want to see first thing in the morning. Lise Arsenault and Matt Walker, tongue wrestling.

They were described around school as an "item." Obviously not an item of good taste.

The bell rang. It was as if the switch on an electromagnet had been flipped, only instead of metal objects, it was kids who were pulled inexorably toward the double front doors. Another day in paradise. Or, as we used to say back home, *ça commence encore*.

That day, for the first time since I had set foot in East Hastings Regional High, I was acutely aware of Peter Flosnick, which was odd, because I had managed to survive almost all of my first six weeks without giving him a single thought. When Ms. Michaud read out his name in homeroom, I looked around and saw nothing but indifference reflected in face after face. Nobody seemed to care whether Peter was there to say "Present" or whether his name was followed by silence, signifying absence. Even Ms. Michaud didn't pause longer than it took to glance for confirmation at his empty seat. If anyone in the room was thinking, gee, I wonder where Peter is today, they gave no sign of it. Probably in all of East Hastings only two people cared what had happened to him — his mother, who had called the police, and Levesque, who headed up the police force and was, therefore, responsible for finding him. Poor Peter.

Listen to me. Don't be such a hypocrite, I told myself sternly. If I ever thought about Peter Flosnick before today, it was only to think what a nerd he was. You can't have such a low opinion of a guy, and then march out an air of superiority when you find yourself the only person who seems to notice when something happens to him. When something *maybe* happens, I amended, because for all anyone knew, he could have stolen a car and gone joy-riding, or run away from home, or maybe bribed someone to score some beer or some hard stuff for him and gotten fall-down drunk and passed out somewhere, and maybe he's waking up right this minute with a gigantic headache.

Forget Peter Flosnick, I told myself.

* * *

That night after Mom and Phoebe were in bed, I sat up, supposedly reading, but really waiting. It was nearly midnight before I heard the car in the driveway, then the footsteps on the graveled path that led to the front door. I swung off the bed to the sound of Levesque's keys dropping onto the little table in the front hall. As I tiptoed down the stairs I heard the fridge door open and then close again. Levesque was pouring himself a glass of milk when I entered the kitchen. A bold black eyebrow arched as he glanced from me to the clock on the stove and back at me again.

"Up late studying?" he said. I couldn't tell if it was a serious question or if that annoyingly amused look meant that he suspected I'd been up doing my nails or poring over a teen magazine or something equally frivolous. I could never tell. It drove me crazy sometimes.

"I have a history test tomorrow," I told him.

He nodded and gulped down half of his glass of milk. He wasn't going to volunteer anything. I don't know what had made me think he might. If I wanted to know, I was going to have to ask.

"So," I said, trying to sound casual, "did you find him?"

"Find who?"

"Peter Flosnick."

He drained the rest of the milk from the glass.

"You know I don't discuss police business at home."

I didn't have to be a member of the police detective brotherhood to figure out what that meant.

"So where was he?"

Levesque peered at me for a moment with those coal-black eyes of his. Then he said, "In the park, at MacAdam's Lookout."

MacAdam's Lookout is a cliff. A dizzyingly high cliff. It seems some guy named Jock MacAdam was the first white man to stand on that particular spot and gaze out over what is now East Hastings Provincial Park. The lookout is solid rock, a big, bare slab of Canadian Shield that sticks out like an old man's bald head up above a forest of pine and spruce and birch. There was a certain logic to Peter being there. A guy who loved stars, out in the park, away from the lights of town, where you could get a really good look at the night sky.

"Star-gazing, I bet," I said.

Levesque shook his head. "He was at the bottom of the lookout, not the top."

That didn't make any sense. "What was he doing there?"

This earned me another long look from Levesque. "I'm sorry to say, he wasn't breathing."

# Chapter 2

It's funny how something terrible can happen to someone, and yet the whole rest of the world goes clicking along as if nothing has happened at all. Okay, so maybe funny isn't the right word. Maybe what I mean is, it's sad. It's as if everyone who isn't directly affected is insensitive to what's going on inside that one pocket of misery. Peter Flosnick had taken a nose dive off MacAdam's Lookout. The police — with Levesque in the lead — were trying to piece together his last hours and minutes. His mother was making arrangements to bury her only child. And all around her, people went about their normal routines. Even me. After all, Peter hadn't been my friend. He had barely registered on my radar. If he had moved to another town or even another country, I wouldn't have cared.

So why did something get under my skin in the days that followed his suicide? That was the official verdict — suicide. As far as anyone was able to determine, Peter's flight had been self-propelled. Why did that get to me the way it did? I got angry when Mr. Markle said, "Science quiz on Monday, so study up, folks," as if, of course, we would do exactly that, because, let's face it, science was more important to our futures than Peter's death. It made me want to punch my fist through a wall when Ms. Peters reminded us that twenty percent of our term grade depended on our participation on the school paper or the school journal or the school yearbook ("So, those of you have haven't signed up had better do so before I make the assignments."), as if that twenty percent loomed larger in our lives than the tragedy of one more teen suicide. It made me want to snarl at Phoebe when I came home after school and found her composing and then testing out cheers for the school football team. Cheers! I went up to my room and slammed the door. A strange, gangly, amateur star man had been so miserable and depressed that he had taken his own life, and no one except his mother seemed to care.

It got to me. Strange, huh?

A guy I had never given a second thought to during his lifetime filled my thoughts after his death. I thought, for example, about that weird moment after math class about a week ago. I had just walked out of class. I looked down the hall and saw Thomas Rennie coming toward me. Call me shallow, call me superficial, but the guy made me drool. I don't think there's a person not on a movie screen who's as handsome as Thomas Rennie. He has deep blue eyes, masses of black curly hair, the straightest teeth I've ever seen outside of a pair of braces, and a lean, hard-looking, football player body. He was coming down the hall directly toward me. He smiled at me, then raised a hand to wave at me. At least, that's what I thought he was doing. I should have known better. I should have known my brain wasn't processing the information correctly. If it had been, it would have flashed a warning, something like, *since when has Mr. Gorgeous given any indication that he even knows you're alive?*

But my brain didn't do that. I saw Thomas raise his hand to wave. I raised mine to wave back. Almost immediately I saw his face change. First he looked puzzled. Then his great big grin was replaced with what can only be called a pity smile. He nodded at me, then dismissed me. I glanced over my shoulder and almost died on the spot. He had raised his arm not to wave at me but at someone *behind* me, at Lise Arsenault and Daria Dattillo, the Empty-Headed Queens. That figured. Thomas was friends with Matt, who was going out with Lise. It wouldn't have surprised me to discover that Thomas was going with Daria. They made a nice, cozy foursome. That's when I turned and saw Peter Flosnick staring at me. And what was that I read in his eyes? It looked like sympathy. Sympathy and something else. Solidarity, maybe. What was that all about?

Peter popped into my head again when I was hurrying to history class. I was halfway down the main floor hall when I heard a cry of anguish: "My keys! Where are my keys?"

I looked around and saw Lise pulling clothes and books and papers out of her locker and thrusting them into the already overburdened arms of her friend Daria. Her frantic rummaging made me stop and stare. I was thinking of Peter. When was it? Last Friday? The day before that? I'd been walking along the second floor hall and I'd seen Peter Flosnick ripping through his locker, just like Lise was doing now, throwing things out of it — books, papers, old lunch bags, magazines, wadded up gym socks — pitching it all out. I couldn't help it. I found myself wondering what he was looking for. It was none of my business, of course, and I continued on by. I would have slipped past unnoticed, too, if a paperback hadn't suddenly struck me on the ear.

"Hey!" I yelled. "Watch it, will you?" Now, when I thought about it, I realized that those were the last words I ever spoke to Peter Flosnick.

Peter stopped his rooting as if he had been flash-frozen. It seemed to take forever before he turned to look at me, and when he did, his chest slowly fell as all the air seeped out of his lungs. His eyes seemed to say, it's only you. He looked at the book at my feet.

"Sorry," he said.

I picked up the book, a well-thumbed volume of short stories by Edgar Allan Poe, and handed it to him. He nodded but said nothing.

"What are you looking at?" Daria Dattillo demanded now, startling me out of my thoughts about Peter. Daria's arms were piled so high with all the books and papers that Lise had heaped onto her that she had to strain to see over them, but that didn't stop her from drilling into me with her steely gray eyes. Lise was on her knees now, rummaging in the bottom of her locker. She didn't even look up at me.

"Nothing," I said, and walked away.

* * *

Two days after Peter's body was found, I reported for duty at the newspaper. When it came to picking my poison, English assignment-wise, I didn't have much of a choice. Phoebe had volunteered — volunteered! — to work on the yearbook, which pretty much canceled that option for me. The literary journal was a magnet for every black-clad, would-be poet in East Hastings and environs, and, from what I had seen from back issues, most of them would be would-bes forever. If there's anything I can't stand, it's people who think they can but who really can't. That left the newspaper, which occupied an office in the basement of the school a few steps away from the boiler room.

I knocked on the door. No one answered. I hesitated, then tried the doorknob. It turned, so I pushed it open.

They say Las Vegas is lit so brightly all around the clock that you can't tell day from night. The newspaper office was like that too, to compensate for the lack of windows, I guess. A dozen office desks sat aligned neatly in three rows of four. Half of them were occupied. Off to one side was a door marked Darkroom — Do Not Enter. Beside it was another door marked Editor. It was open and I saw a guy inside sitting in front of a monitor. He

16

glanced at me, then leapt to his feet and charged toward me.

"Hi," he said, thrusting out a hand. His face was long and thin — his whole body was long and thin — but his smile was broad and seemed genuine. "I'm Ross Jenkins. Editor."

"Chloe Yan."

Ross nodded. "I know. Ms. Peters told me to expect you. She said you're a terrific writer."

I tried to hide my surprise. I was doing well enough in English. But a "terrific" writer?

"Too bad we don't have a crime beat," Ross said. "I guess you'd be a natural. But Ms. Peters makes us stick to school news and student issues."

"Excuse me?" I said. I gave him one of my patented, guaranteed-to-wither-grapes-into-raisins looks. "I don't think I follow you."

"It's in our guidelines. Our mandate, Ms. Peters calls it. Our mandate is to cover all the news that matters to students." He spoke as if he were reciting a soliloquy from Shakespeare, only minus the poetry. "Those last three words are the key — "

I waved him silent. "I mean, why did you say I'd be a natural on the crime beat?" He obviously had a mistaken impression of me. I intended to set him straight.

"Your dad *is* chief of police, right?" Ross said, grinning. "Talk about having great sources."

I moved up close to Ross Jenkins, Editor, until my nose almost touched his. When I spoke, I kept my voice low, a little trick I had learned from

Levesque. If you talk quietly, it forces the other guy to listen hard, and people generally pay more attention to something they have to work at hearing. This gives the speaker an edge of authority.

"I'm going to say this once and only once," I told him. "First of all, he's not my father, he's my stepfather. Second — and the more important thing for you to remember — what he does has nothing to do with me. You got that? I'm me, I do what I do, and he's him, and whether he's the chief of police, the undertaker or the garbage man doesn't make any difference to anything in my life. Okay?"

Ross's head was bobbing like a clown head on a jack-in-the-box spring before I got halfway through my speech.

"I'm sorry," he said. "I didn't mean anything by it."

I glowered at him. I was angry that he'd made me lose my cool. I spent a lot of time telling myself I didn't care who my mother was married to. It was none of my business. But this was a small town, and Levesque *was* chief of police. It was like having the local church minister as your father. Or the guy who ran the municipal dump. You might not want it to matter, but it did. People made all kinds of assumptions. They decided things about you, including how much they wanted to get to know you — or not — based on things like that, things that had nothing to do with your life and what you did with it. It made me furious. And it made me even more furious that now someone knew *how* furious it made me.

"Just forget it," I said.

"Okay, consider it forgotten." He was smiling wider than ever to show he meant no harm. "Come on. I'll show you to your desk."

He led me to one that was unoccupied. Well, unoccupied, but hardly uncluttered.

"We're at least two to a desk down here," he said. "But you're guaranteed your own drawer. Ta-da!" He yanked open the bottom drawer. His smile slipped when he saw its jumbled interior. "Oops, sorry. I guess whoever had this drawer at the end of last year forgot to clean it out." He reached in and pulled out a few sheets of paper. His already serious expression turned somber.

"Problem?" I asked.

It took him a moment to pull his attention away from the papers in his hand.

"It's Anna Maria's stuff," he said. "I guess nobody had the heart to throw it out."

"Anna Maria?" I had no idea who he was talking about.

"Anna Maria Dattillo."

"As in, related to Daria Dattillo?" I asked. Daria Dattillo, Lise Arsenault and her boyfriend Matt Walker — he of tongue-wrestling fame — and Thomas Rennie were East Hastings Regional's aristocracy. Lise Arsenault's father managed one of the two mines that were still open. I'm not sure what Matt Walker's dad did, but I do know that he had money. Lots of it. The Dattillo family lived in a big house on the lake. And Thomas — well,

Thomas was mesmerizing. Not just because he was great looking and not just because he was athletic, although that didn't hurt. It was his bounce. His buoyancy. The sparkle in his eyes. The ease with which he smiled. The only trouble was, he never smiled at me. He paid me no attention at all. None of them did.

Ross nodded in response to my question.

"She was a good writer," he said with admiration. "And a good poet. It turns out that talent for poetry runs in the Dattillo family. I heard her sister is also pretty good."

"Her sister? You don't mean Daria?" I had fallen into the habit of thinking of Daria and her friend Lise as the Empty-Headed Queens, the Princesses of Giggle. I didn't know they took anything seriously, except maybe the crucial and apparently endlessly fascinating subjects of clothes, makeup and boys.

Ross nodded. "You know her?"

"I thought everyone in school knew her."

"According to Ms. Peters, the whole world is going to know her one day. She's already had a couple of poems published in a literary journal. And I don't mean the journal here at school. I mean a real one."

It was a monumental, uphill battle to imagine one of the Empty-Headed Queens with a genuine thought in her head, especially one worth publishing.

"So," I said, "what's the deal with her sister? You said nobody had the heart to throw out her stuff.

What do you mean?"

"Anna Maria was killed in a car accident last year." He sighed. "I guess it's about time someone cleaned this drawer out, though. Feel free." He let the papers in his hand fall back into the drawer. "We're having a staff meeting in fifteen minutes. See you then, okay?"

As he walked back to his office, I pulled out the chair and dropped down onto it. I fished out a sheaf of papers from the drawer and flipped through them. They looked like notes of some kind. At first I thought maybe they were notes for a newspaper article, but nothing made sense. I flipped through page after page of big, loopy handwriting until it finally clicked. Jazz June, silver-gray moon. Sharp white light, deep, dead night. These were poem notes. Not very good ones, either, if you want my opinion. But I guess it wasn't fair to judge an unfinished poem on the basis of a bunch of loopy notes. I gathered up everything in the drawer and looked around for the nearest wastebasket. It was garbage, right?

"Hey, finally," said a voice behind me. I spun around to face a short, stocky boy with a buzz cut. He grinned. "Eric Moore," he said. "Top drawer."

"Chloe Yan. Bottom drawer."

"Finally getting rid of all that poetry crap, huh? Terrific."

"You don't like poetry?"

"You kidding? I'm the sports editor." He obviously considered this sufficient explanation because he didn't elaborate.

I shuffled through a few more pages and wondered what Anna Maria Dattillo's poetry sounded like when it was polished. Maybe it was good, maybe it wasn't, but from all these notes it was clear that a lot of work had gone into them. Who was I to pass judgment? I tucked the papers back into the drawer and pushed it shut with my foot. I wasn't ready to pitch out someone's life work.

\* \* \*

The next day I went to Peter's funeral. When you go to a kid's funeral, you expect to see more kids there than adults. That wasn't the case with Peter Flosnick. There was a reasonably good-sized delegation from East Hastings Regional, including Ross Jenkins and a few others from the newspaper, and, to my surprise, the Empty-Headed Queens and their consorts, Matt and Thomas. But most of the church was filled with adults. Some of them I knew — our immediate neighbors, for example, and some teachers from East Hastings. The man who ran the flower shop near the police station was there too. I recognized him because Levesque had sent me over there on Mom's birthday to order flowers. He couldn't do it himself because he was heading out with a couple of dozen men from town looking for a toddler who had wandered away from a campsite in the park. I also recognized one of the librarians from the public library.

I went to the funeral on my own and found a seat near the back of the church. But I wasn't on my own for long. Before the service started Levesque slipped into the pew next to me. He didn't say anything. He just sat there beside me, a big, bulky man in a dark suit, looking appropriately somber.

After the service everyone filed out of the church past Mrs. Flosnick. Her eyes were red from crying. Standing next to her, squeezing her hand and supplying her with fresh tissues, was a woman in a navy blue suit. As Levesque and I joined the line I saw Lise Arsenault shoot an angry look at this woman, then march right out of the church without stopping to say anything to Mrs. Flosnick. What was that all about? I wondered.

"If looks could kill, huh?" said a voice behind me. Ross Jenkins. I turned around and gave him a sharp look. He immediately turned red in the face. "Bad choice of words," he muttered. "Sorry."

"Who is she?" I asked.

"Who?"

"That woman Lise was glowering at."

"Eileen Braden," Ross said. "She used to teach at East Hastings."

It was apparent from Lise's expression that she had not been this teacher's pet.

"What happened?" I asked. "Did she throw a few failing grades Lise's way?"

Levesque shot me a stern look, and I clamped my mouth shut. We were only one person away from Mrs. Flosnick. Immediately in front of us was the man from the flower shop.

"I'm so sorry about what happened," he was saying to Mrs. Flosnick. "Peter was a good boy and a hard worker. I've missed having him around the shop these past months."

Mrs. Flosnick looked puzzled. "What do you mean?" she said.

The flower shop man seemed flustered. "What do I mean?"

"You said you missed him in the past months? Wasn't Peter showing up for work?"

The flower shop man's face turned pinkish. "I thought you knew," he said. "Peter quit. He told me he didn't need the money anymore."

That sounded to me like classic suicide behavior. We studied the symptoms in health class last year. People who were depressed and considering the ultimate option often made radical changes in their behavior — they withdrew from activities, they gave away favorite possessions, they decided they didn't need things anymore, things like money. Maybe Mrs. Flosnick knew this, too, because her eyes flooded with tears. Eileen Braden pressed a wad of tissues into her hand. Mrs. Flosnick was crying so hard by the time Levesque and I reached her that the best I could do was mutter my condolences. I was glad to get out of the church. I was glad, too, that Levesque was there with me, because after I stammered out a few words he took one of Mrs. Flosnick's hands into his and held it for a moment. It seemed to calm her. She looked up at him, straightening, composing herself. Then she said, "Thank you so much for coming. Thank you for everything." He had that effect on people. There was a tranquility about him that was soothing and — I hate to admit it — comforting. It almost made me understand why Mom married him.

As we walked together to his car we passed Lise and her entourage.

"I hate her," she was saying, with real feeling. "I hate her and I hate what she did to my father."

Who, I wondered? Eileen Braden? What could she possibly have done to Lise's father?

# Chapter 3

The next day I arrived home to an empty house. Phoebe was still at school, debating or cheering or editing — I didn't know which, and I didn't care. Mom was at work. She had taken a part-time job as a cashier at the Canadian Tire store down on Dundas Street. She had also enrolled in some courses at the community college up in Morrisville. Levesque was at work too. This gave me the chance to have a nice, long, uninterrupted bubble bath. At least, that was my plan. The doorbell rang just as I was getting ready to hop in. Ignore it, I told myself. After all, it wasn't as if anyone knew I was here.

The doorbell rang again.

I pulled off both shoes.

It rang again.

Then whoever was out there leaning on the bell must have decided it was broken because he — or she — started to hammer on the door.

This had better be important, I thought as I thumped down the stairs. And it sure had better not be Phoebe with some lame excuse about how she had lost her keys again. I wrenched open the front door, prepared to rip into her.

"Oh, excuse me," said the flustered-looking woman standing on the front porch. With her pale blue belted dress, sensible shoes, middle-aged perm and little black handbag, Mrs. Flosnick looked as if she had stepped out of a nineteen fifties movie. "I was told this is where the police chief lives."

"It is, but — "

"I went up to the police station," she said. She spoke softly but quickly. "I'm sorry," she said, "I don't mean to bother you. I know the chief probably doesn't like to be pestered at home." She was falling all over herself apologizing for being on our porch, and yet here she was. In my opinion, if people didn't go around doing what their better judgment obviously told them not to do, they would save themselves a lot of breath. "Really, it would never have occurred to me to come here like this. It's just that — "

"He isn't here," I said. I admit that I was a little short-tempered, but all I could think was that my bath was cooling fast and all my bubbles were probably popping away. And besides, there was nothing I could do to help her. I also admit that I interrupted her, which was rude, and that my voice wasn't as soft and apologetic as hers. But even so, I didn't expect her to start crying, which is exactly what she did. Her lips started quivering, a tear trickled down her cheek, and she groped in her little black handbag for some tissues, which, of course, she had — a neat little plastic package of them. Then suddenly I was the one who was apologizing, even though, when I thought the whole thing over later, I was

27

pretty sure that she had overreacted. It wasn't as if I had slammed the door in her face.

"He's over in Campbellford," I told her. "He should be back — " With Levesque, in his line of work, you never knew. "He'll definitely be back sometime," I said. "I'm sure if you leave a message for him — " I had been going to say, leave a message for him at the police station, but she didn't give me a chance to finish.

"I'm Elizabeth Flosnick," she said. "Peter Flosnick's mother?" She said it as if it were a question, as if she wasn't sure anymore. Can you be someone's mother when that person no longer existed?

"I'm Chloe," I said. "Lev — Louis Levesque is my stepfather."

"Chloe?" She peered at me. "You were at the funeral, weren't you?"

I nodded.

"Peter talked about you a lot." Her face softened into something close to a smile. "He liked you. You two must have been good friends."

If Peter Flosnick and I had been friends at all, let alone good ones, it was news to me. I opened my mouth to contradict her, but changed my mind. If I told her the truth — that I barely knew Peter — she might get upset all over again, and I didn't want to be responsible for that. Besides, what difference did it make now what Peter had told his mother? It was all in the past. So I just smiled at her and said nothing.

"I know what your father thinks," she said. "I know what the official police position is. I even agreed with it at the beginning. It seemed like the only possible explanation. Peter isn't — wasn't — " Tears reappeared, and she dabbed them away with a tissue. "He wasn't foolhardy. One way it could have happened was if Peter had been hanging out over the lookout. But he would never have taken a chance like that. So it couldn't have been an accident. I was convinced of that right off and I'm still convinced. And if it wasn't an accident, well then, it had to be the other, didn't it?" By "the other," she meant suicide. "That's what the police concluded, and they're the professionals, aren't they? They deal with this sort of thing all the time." She trembled a little — shuddered, really — the way people do when they think of coroners and morticians, people who see death every day, people who *handle* it. Then she shook her head. "I agreed with what the police told me because I couldn't think of any alternative."

What about the suicide note? I wanted to ask, but I didn't have the nerve. Levesque had said that a neatly typed note had been fished out of Peter's pocket.

"I've had a good, hard think about it," Mrs. Flosnick said. "And I know that my Peter would never have done such a thing. You tell the police chief that for me. Tell him, Peter Flosnick's mother doesn't care what they found in his pocket, she knows for a fact that her son would never do such a thing. Tell him I'd stake my own life on it. That's my message." She had changed completely by now. No more tears. No more apologies. No more soft and powdery, old-fashioned appearance. She stood straight and tall now, and seemed hard and determined, all steel and grit. "You'll tell him, won't you?"

I promised I would.

I kept my word to Mrs. Flosnick. I delivered her message to Levesque that night over dinner.

"The poor woman," my mother said. "It must be so hard to accept something like that."

"I don't get it," Phoebe said. "If she doesn't think his death was an accident and she doesn't think it was suicide, what does she think happened?"

"Maybe she thinks there was a second shooter," I said.

Everyone stared at me.

"Like the Kennedy assassination," I said. They kept right on staring. "It's a joke," I said.

"I don't think you should be joking about a thing like this," my mother said. Her tone of voice and the look she gave me were pretty effective. I felt embarrassed and muttered an apology.

"Seriously," Phoebe said. "What does she think?"

"She didn't tell me," I said.

"I wasn't talking to you. I was talking to Dad."

My mother got a soft, gooey look in her eyes when Phoebe said that. She loved to hear Levesque referred to as Dad. I guess she thought that meant he was accepted.

"I didn't speak to her, Phoebe," Levesque said mildly.

"Yes, but — "

"For someone with such a good grade point average, you can be really stupid, Pheebs," I said. "Don't you know there are only four ways to check out? Sickness, suicide, accident and on purpose."

"On purpose?" My perfect little sister looked completely baffled. "You mean . . . ?"

"Peter's mother thinks someone did him in." I looked at Levesque. "She thinks he was murdered, doesn't she?"

Levesque said nothing.

* * *

The next day when I reported to the school paper, Eric Moore, the sports editor, seemed to be in the grips of some kind of shaking sickness. His head kept wagging back and forth.

"I can't believe it," he said. "A thousand dollars. They actually paid her a thousand dollars for a grand total of two hundred words. That's five dollars a word! I bet even *Sports Illustrated* doesn't pay five dollars a word."

"It's a prestigious publication," said Brenda Plunkett, editor of the school literary journal. "Okay, sure, it's a *student* contest. But anyone who's anyone in the literary world reads *Poetry Now*. And you know what? I heard that the winner of the contest a couple of years ago had her first collection of poetry published when she was still in university."

Andrea Thompson, who also worked on the school journal, said, "Anna Maria entered that contest the year she — " She broke off and changed course. "She didn't even get honorable mention."

"What's going on?" I asked Ross. He filled me in. And once he had, I did a pretty fair imitation of Eric.

"Let me get this straight," I said. There was always a chance I had heard incorrectly. "You're telling me that Daria Dattillo" — Empty-Headed Queen Daria Dattillo — "won first prize in the most prestigious student poetry contest in the country?" I peered at Ross. "Is that what you're telling me?"

"That's what I'm telling you," he said.

"And it will make a great story for the paper," said Ms. Peters. Where had she come from? I was pretty sure she hadn't been there when I walked in. Or had she? "Chloe, I'm assigning this one to you. I want you to interview Daria, talk to her about her winning entry, her plans to pursue poetry — "

"Me?" I said. The thought of interviewing one of the Empty-Headed Queens was . . . well . . . humiliating. "I haven't read her poem. I'm not familiar with *Poetry Now*. I don't even know all that much about poetry." That wasn't one hundred percent true. I knew as much as any other high school kid, I liked some of what I knew, and I even had a few favorite poems and poets. But that didn't mean I had any interest in interviewing Daria Dattillo about her triumph.

"I can't think of a better way to learn about a subject than to talk to an expert," Ms. Peters said. She handed me a magazine. I glanced at the cover: *Poetry Now.*

"I don't suppose there's any chance you'd let me do a different story instead?" I said.

Ms. Peters shook her head. "I'm the assignment editor. Consider yourself assigned."

\* \* \*

"No," Daria said. She slammed her locker shut.

I am not going to beg, I told myself. I am not going to plead with one of the Empty-Headed Queens to let me interview her while a second Empty-Headed Queen smirks at me from the sidelines. But Ms. Peters had made herself clear. A good reporter takes whatever assignment is handed to her. A good reporter adapts to the situation, unearths all the pertinent facts, and is not swayed by personal preference or prejudice. "Take the assignment and stop arguing with me, Chloe," she had said. "It's the mature thing to do." Which meant that if, for whatever reason, I failed to get the story, I would also have failed the Lorna Peters maturity test. There was no way in this world that Daria Dattillo or any other little Queen was going to make me do that.

"Look," I said to Daria, "if you turn me down, the only thing that's going to happen is that Ms. Peters is going to put her head together with Ms. Martin," who, besides being vice-principal, was a close friend of Ms. Peters, "and the two of them are going to pressure you until you agree to let the school paper do a story about you. This is a big deal to them. You can't fight it." At least, you couldn't fight Ms. Peters. Well, you could *fight* her, but you couldn't expect to *win*. "So why not make it easy on everyone and let me do an interview? Thirty minutes tops. After school. What do you say?"

Daria glanced at Lise, who shrugged.

"You know what they say, Dare. Don't do the crime if you can't do the time. You wrote the poem. You let Ms. Peters enter it in the contest. You owe it to your public to tell your story." She was treating it like it was all a big joke. Some friend.

Daria still looked undecided. "Thirty minutes," she said at last. "Meet me here."

* * *

I was just coming out of math class on my way to history, a pile of textbooks and two thick binders clutched to my chest. I was walking fast, hoping to get to class in time to do a quick review of my notes before my test, when I saw something in the corridor that brought me to a screeching halt. I peered at the sight. Yup, it was him all right, loping down the hall beside Ms. Jeffries, the principal. He was hunched over slightly to bring his ear closer to her. Ms. Jeffries was small, barely more than five feet. She hardly came up to Levesque's shoulder. But what was he doing here?

He was getting closer now, and although his complete attention seemed focused on Ms. Jeffries, I ducked back a little, to make sure he didn't see me. If I had been serious about not being seen, I thought later, I probably should have jumped out a window. The whole time I was watching Levesque, he seemed one hundred percent absorbed in what Ms. Jeffries was saying, one hundred percent focused on her compact body and no-nonsense face. But the minute I took a step back, his eyes came up and away from Ms. Jeffries, cut through all the heads and faces in the crowded corridor, and zeroed right in on me. He looked at me. He nodded at me. Then, mercifully, he kept right on going. What was he doing here? I wondered again.

\* \* \*

I was surprised to find Daria waiting at her locker after school, as arranged. I was even more surprised to find her alone.

"I thought we could go down to the newspaper office," I said. The truth was, I hadn't really thought about it at all. I hadn't expected her to show up.

Daria shook her head. "Let's go in here," she said.

Here was an empty classroom. Daria went directly to the middle of it and sat down at one of the desks. I pulled up a chair and sat across from her. Then I took the tape recorder from my bag.

"This okay?" I asked.

Daria stared at it as if it were a poisonous snake, rattling and ready to strike. In the end, though, she nodded.

I opened my notebook. I had jotted down a series

of questions, none of them particularly brilliant. I liked to write. It was one of the few things in school that I did reasonably well. But so far in my life I had written exactly zero newspaper articles and had conducted an equal number of interviews. Daria didn't have to know that, though.

"How long have you been writing poetry?" I asked after I had turned on the tape recorder. Okay, so it was a lame opener. But you have to start somewhere, right?

She squirmed in her seat and looked down at the desktop. Then she said, "A couple of years."

"Is this the first poem of yours that's been published?"

Her head swung up. She gave me a sharp look. "I've had seven poems published in the school journal and two in the yearbook last year." Her tone made it clear that any halfway decent reporter should have known this, because any half-decent reporter would have done her homework.

"Are you planning to be a poet — ?" I stopped suddenly. I'd almost asked, are you planning to be a poet when you grow up? Groan. Quickly, I rephrased. "Are you planning to pursue a career in poetry?"

"No," Daria said. Sharp. Sudden. Just like that. Then, after a moment, "I haven't really decided what I'm going to do."

"Your sister wrote pretty good poetry, too, didn't she?" I said.

More signs of irritation. "So?"

"So, it's interesting to find two good poets in one family. My kid sister isn't anything like me. We don't have anything in common."

"I don't think I understand your point."

I wasn't even sure that I had one. The interview wasn't going well. Daria was answering each question as briefly as possible. I decided to take another approach.

"Tell me about 'Autumn Sunset,'" I said. That was the name of the poem that had won the *Poetry Now* prize. "Tell me how that poem came about."

Daria stiffened. "You can't talk about how a poem comes about," she said. "It just does. It just happens."

"I really liked it," I said. I had promised myself I wasn't going to say that. This was an Empty-Headed Queen, after all. Daria and her friend Lise floated around the school on their own separate little clouds, high above everyone else. They looked down on other kids. To compliment one of them was to encourage their outrageously superior attitude. Still . . . "It worked so well on two levels. The first time I read it, I thought, wow, this is such a beautiful description of an autumn night, all the yellows and oranges and rose colors in the sky, and the whole time you know the nights, the black times, are getting longer and longer, and the sunsets are getting less beautiful, less spectacular. Then I read it again, and it suddenly hit me, this is a life. A beautiful, vital life, in decline. It was really well done."

Daria listened in silence. Tears welled up in her

eyes, and she pushed them away roughly, almost angrily.

"What do you want me to say?" she said. "What I wrote was how I felt. I watched the sun go down one night, and it reminded me of my grandmother, who loved to watch the sunset. She could describe all the sunsets she had seen. It was as if she was talking about snowflakes. No two of them were alike. Each one had special characteristics that made it stand out from all the others. I tried to write about one sunset I had seen. I tried to describe it as if I were my grandmother, and — I don't know — I just found myself writing about her."

"What did your parents say when you told them you'd won the contest? They must have been very proud of you. I understand that your sister entered the same contest and didn't even get an honorable mention — "

Daria looked sharply at me. "My sister has nothing to do with this." She gathered her things and stood up.

"Look, I didn't mean anything." It had been a stupid question. Her sister had died a little over a year ago. Obviously the tragedy was still fresh in Daria's mind. "I'm sorry. Please don't go. I still have a few more questions."

"Well, I have no more answers," Daria said.

Dumb, dumb, dumb, I thought as I watched Daria sweep from the room. This time, though, I was referring to myself.

* * *

I sat in front of a computer in the newspaper office and read over the notes I had transcribed from my interview with Daria. When I finished, I read them over again — and again.

"Problem?" Ross Jenkins leaned over and glanced at the screen.

"Rotten interview."

"She didn't have anything to say?"

"It wasn't her. It was me. I really blew it. I said all the wrong things."

"Like?"

"Like, she just started to open up a little and tell me what she thought about when she wrote that prize-winning poem, and I said something about her sister and, bang, she slammed the door shut on me. Walked right out of the room."

"So?" Ross shrugged. "Talk to her again."

"I think she made it clear that she isn't interested in talking to me."

"If Woodward and Bernstein had taken that attitude, they never would have cracked the Watergate story. Some reporters have to chase subjects for months, even years, before they get the interviews they need to tell a story. You can't take no for an answer."

"I think she hates me."

"I think you're afraid of her."

"I am not."

"You ticked her off. You touched a nerve with her. You hurt her, and when she got angry, you got scared off."

"I am not afraid of her, Ross."

"Well, if you're sitting there with no story because you blew an interview, you must be afraid of something. Because if you weren't, you'd be hounding her for a second chance. No interview, no story, right?"

What a lousy day. First it turned out that one of the insufferable Empty-Headed Queens didn't have such an empty head after all. And now Ross was giving me advice that, much to my annoyance, was actually good. But if I admitted that, I would have to take the next step and do for a second time what I had promised myself I wouldn't do at all in the first place — I would have to beg Daria Dattillo for an interview again. I snapped my notebook shut.

"Okay, okay," I said.

"Hey, guess what? I talked to your stepfather today," Ross said suddenly.

I looked sharply at him. "What about?"

"Peter Flosnick. He was in the school almost all afternoon, talking to kids about Peter."

"What for? Peter's death was a suicide."

Ross shrugged. "He was asking if Peter seemed depressed. Had he been acting out of the ordinary? Stuff like that. I liked him. He seemed like a nice guy."

"Peter?"

"No, your stepfather."

"Why was he talking to *you* about Peter?" I asked. "I didn't know you and he were friends."

"Friends? No. But Peter wrote an astronomy column for the paper. And I am the editor. And you know how popular his column was."

I looked at him blankly.

He shook his head in disgust. "It's so nice to know that the people who work here take an interest in what goes on. Peter's column ran in almost a dozen school papers."

"I heard that. But it was popular?"

Ross nodded. "And he got lots of mail. He was always writing to some professor in Toronto he met at a science fair, and the professor always wrote back. And he got mail from little kids — he wrote an amateur star-gazing column for a kids' magazine. It's called 'Star Corner.'" He nodded to a set of mail slots mounted on the wall. One of them was bulging with envelopes of all sizes. "I'm not sure what to do with all of that. Any ideas?"

I shook my head.

He stared at the mail slots for a moment before turning back to me. "So," he said, "do you want to do a little role playing? I'll be Daria, you can be the groveling reporter, and we'll figure out the best way to humiliate you so that Daria will jump at the chance to answer your questions. What do you say?"

\* \* \*

I almost knocked Thomas Rennie over. I almost broke his nose with the door, too, as I plowed it open and barreled through it.

"I'm sorry," I said. Was that pain I saw on his

41

face, or only surprise? "Are you all right?"

He had jumped back a pace, and now seemed to be working at composing himself.

"I'm fine," he said. "Hey, is Eric in the office?"

I shook my head. "Ross is there. And Angus MacDougall. And Jane Smythe. That's about it."

He looked disappointed, but only shrugged. "Guess it will have to wait," he said.

"I guess," I said, without knowing exactly what he was talking about. Probably something that Eric had written or was planning to write about the football team. Whatever it was, it was none of my business. I stepped around him and headed for the stairs. To my surprise, he fell into step beside me.

"So," he said, "you're the top cop's kid, right?"

If he had been anyone else, I could have clobbered him. But he was Thomas (sigh!) Rennie and he was talking to me, about me.

"Yeah," I said.

"I've seen you around," he said, "but I haven't seen you at any games."

"I'm not much of a sports fan," I said.

"Oh," he said. "Is that because you hold the traditional girl view of sports or the liberated feminist view?" When I stared at him, trying to figure out what he was talking about, he smiled and explained. "You know: I'm a girl, I'd rather go shopping than go to some boring old football game. Or: I'm a girl — er, woman — and I'm not going to waste my time watching a bunch of macho guys chase a ball around a muddy field, I've got more important things to do, things that genuinely interest me."

I couldn't help it, I laughed. "A combination of both, I guess. Most sports don't interest me. And I've got enough other stuff that I want to do that I don't really have time to waste on things that score low on the riveting scale." I glanced at him. "No offense."

"None taken," he said. Then, "Have you ever considered a career in the diplomatic corps?"

I laughed again. We had reached the exit door. He held it open for me.

"I go this way," he said, nodding north.

"I'm the other way."

"Well, then, I guess I'll see you around." He offered me a friendly smile.

"Yeah," I said. "I guess." I was surprised by how happy that possibility made me. I walked home with a bounce in my step.

# Chapter 4

Mom had just passed me the salad when Levesque came through the front door. She jumped to her feet and rushed out into the front hall to greet him. A few moments of silence followed. Phoebe grinned across the table at me. I ignored her. Okay, so they were kissing. Big deal. In the year since they had been married, they'd been acting like a couple of school kids. What else was new?

There was a blush on Mom's cheeks when she came back into the kitchen holding Levesque's hand. He looked happy, but tired, and slumped into his chair. Mom prepared him a plate of food and passed it to me to pass on.

"Chloe says she saw you at school today," she said.

"I heard you were asking about Peter Flosnick," Phoebe added. "How come? I thought you said it was suicide."

"I did," Levesque said. "But I promised his mother I'd ask around."

"Why?" Phoebe asked. "If it was suicide, it was suicide."

"Maybe his mother wants to know why he did it," I pointed out. Phoebe had turned into a know-it-all since we moved here. Back home, she had been a nobody, your classic little — and invisible — frog in a big pond. When we moved here, she managed to reinvent herself. She was City Girl, always telling people, "This is the way we did it in my old school in Montreal . . . " Surprisingly, this worked, and she had been crowned queen of her new social circle. Or maybe it wasn't so surprising. What did fourteen-year-olds know about anything?

Phoebe made a face at me now. "It's no mystery why he did it," she said. "Peter Flosnick was weird. He was creepy. When you're trying to figure out what happened, you start with the most likely possibility, isn't that what police say?"

"You're thinking of doctors," I said, and I knew even before my mother gave me that warning look that my tone was more disparaging than was strictly necessary. But why was it that Phoebe always acted like she knew everything about everything, whereas, in fact, she usually knew nothing at all? The proof was that her face now turned into a giant question mark, which made it a pleasure to explain to her. "When doctors are making a diagnosis, they say, 'If you hear hoofbeats, think horses.'"

"I bet the same thing applies to police work," Phoebe said, all defensive now. She looked at Levesque. "Right?"

"Common sense is never a bad starting point," Levesque said mildly. "But I don't think Peter's mother believes her son was weird, and even if she did — and you could certainly argue that each of us is, in our own way, a little odd — I don't think she would be prepared to think that his eccentricity was the reason he jumped off MacAdam's Lookout."

Phoebe's cheeks turned red. Score one for the big man.

"I thought I might find out something helpful to Mrs. Flosnick if I talked to some of Peter's peers and heard what they had to say," he continued.

"And?" I asked.

He shrugged. "And nothing. Apparently Peter didn't have many friends."

* * *

I stood at the cafeteria door for ten minutes, then five minutes more, and still no Daria. I paced, I fumed, I muttered unkind thoughts. Mostly I blamed myself. Daria might have written a good poem. It might even, by some standards, have been a great poem. But she wasn't Sylvia Plath and the school paper wasn't *Time* magazine. So what was all this media shyness about? Why was Daria making my job so difficult? She had agreed to another interview, so where was she?

Twenty minutes had passed since the agreed-on time, and still she didn't show up. Wake up and smell the coffee, I thought. You've been stood up.

I pushed open the door and stood inside the cafeteria, scanning faces. I finally found one that looked like it could be useful, and headed for it.

Lise Arsenault's lunch and possessions occupied at least three places at a table in the crowded room. Her tray, littered with lunch leavings, sat at one elbow. Her backpack, spilling out its contents, was at her other elbow. She was munching on an apple as she hunched over the table, reading. Studying for our biology midterm, maybe? The notion jarred, as always. It seemed beyond comprehension to me that someone like Lise, whose every spoken word centered on the superficial things in life — clothes, hair, nail polish, appearances, movie stars — could be on the honor roll, which, I had heard, she had been last year. What was it Levesque liked to say? People aren't just one thing. They're complex. Multi-faceted. There were some facets of Lise Arsenault, though, that were just too much for me to swallow.

When I got closer, I saw that Lise was engrossed not in a textbook, but in a magazine. *Vogue*. She must be some kind of genius, I decided, if she could spend virtually all of her time not thinking about schoolwork and still score high marks. People like that are completely irritating.

I stood beside her for a few moments, waiting to be acknowledged. She didn't even look up.

"Excuse me," I said at last.

"Excuse *me*," Lise said, barely glancing at me. "I'm sure you can see that I'm reading. That means I'm busy. And that means it would be rude and inconsiderate to disturb me."

It was an interesting definition of rude, I decided, considering the source.

"I was supposed to meet Daria here," I said. "I'm pretty sure I saw her in school this morning. Do you know where she is?"

Lise tossed her apple core onto the tray with the rest of the remains of her lunch, wiped her fingertips on a paper napkin and looked at me with new interest.

"Why would Daria want to meet with you?" she asked.

The mature thing would have been to ignore where Lise chose to put her emphasis — on the last word. I had never felt so old in my life as I did when I answered her.

"I was supposed to interview her."

"I thought you did that already."

"I'm doing a second interview."

Lise laughed. "In actual fact," she said, "it looks to me like you're *not* doing a second interview."

"Do you know where she is?"

She shook her head.

"Do you know why she's ducking me?"

"Is that what she's doing?" She said this with wide-eyed innocence.

Time to take another tack.

"Did you read her poem?"

"I glanced at it."

"What did you think?"

A shrug. "I'm not really a poetry person. That's Daria's big thing."

"Does she ever talk to you about why she writes, what she thinks about when she writes, that kind of thing?"

Lise sat back in her chair and gazed evenly at

me. "What is this, some kind of interrogation? Because if it is, no comment. I'm not going to talk to you about Daria. It's up to her to speak for herself." She scooped up her backpack and her magazine, and pushed by me, leaving behind the messy remains of her lunch. I stared after her, hoping there was a special place reserved in the next world for Empty-Headed Queens.

"Problem?" someone behind me said.

I turned to face Thomas Rennie.

"I've been stood up."

He managed to look both shocked and sympathetic. "Whoever he is, don't forgive him. Any guy who would stand up a girl like you, well . . . " He shook his head. "That guy is either crazy or stupid, and either way, you don't want to go out with him, am I right?"

"I wasn't stood up by a boyfriend," I informed him. "I was stood up by an interview. A female interview."

"Interview?" He seemed confused by the word. Then, "Oh, you're writing a story for the school paper, is that it?"

I nodded.

"Hey, I have an idea. Why don't you interview me?"

"You? Why? What have you done?"

He feigned offense. "I'm a sports hero."

"I'm not interested in sports, remember?"

Now he looked wounded. "How could I forget? But a guy can always hope, can't he?"

I glanced at the clock on the wall. I still had enough time before my next class to do a quick circuit of the school to see if I could find Daria. Maybe she was ducking me, but if she was in school, she could be found. She wasn't invisible.

Thomas said something. I looked blankly at him.

"I'm sorry, what?"

"I said, are you busy tomorrow? If you're not, maybe we could do something. Go to a movie, maybe. Or to the arcade. You like video games?"

I stared at him. He was asking me out. The star of the football team, who I had told flat out on two separate occasions that I had no interest whatsoever in sports, was asking me out. The incredibly great-looking, charming, and — surprise — funny star of the football team who I had been gazing at from afar ever since I first set foot in East Hastings Regional, was asking me out.

"Sure," I said. I was going for a casual attitude. I don't know if I succeeded. To tell the truth, the only thing I remember clearly after he asked me out was that his deep blue eyes had little flecks of deeper blue in them. I had never seen eyes like that before. A girl could fall in love with a guy with eyes like those.

* * *

I didn't find Daria that day, but I ran smack into her when I showed up a few minutes early for English class the next morning. She was speaking to Ms. Peters when I walked into the room, and they both stopped talking and looked over at me.

50

Then Daria clutched her books to her chest and hurried over to her desk. Ms. Peters said, "May I have a word with you, Chloe?"

I hate that kind of phony politeness. Teachers use it a lot. And vice-principals. Especially vice-principals. *May I have a word with you?* Did I really have a choice? Did she expect me to say, "Terribly sorry, Ms. Peters, but no, you may not?"

"I think you should drop the idea of writing about Daria. She feels uncomfortable with the idea of being profiled," Ms. Peters said. "Not everyone seeks the spotlight, you know. Maybe it would be better if you came up with another subject for your story." She said all of this as if Daria were the new J.D. Salinger, as if the intrusive profile had been my idea, as if I had been pursuing poor reluctant Daria to the ends of the earth, like some fanatic *paparazzo*.

"No problem," I said quickly and loudly enough for Daria to hear. "Like I told you when you suggested the piece, I'm really not into poetry." Then I took my own seat. I didn't even look at Daria.

\* \* \*

"So," Ross said, "what are you going to write about?"

I had no idea. Ms. Peters didn't want me to write about Daria, but she did want me to write about something. She hadn't given me any suggestions, though.

"Thomas Rennie suggested I write about him," I said.

Ross shook his head. "Been done," he said. "Been done to death, right, Eric?"

Eric looked up from his keyboard. "What's that about death?"

"Not death. Thomas Rennie. You think he needs any more coverage in the paper?"

"I wish for once my column didn't mention his name a dozen times," Eric said. "It's getting boring writing about him and I'm sure it's getting boring reading about him. One more reason to mourn Adam Gillette."

"Who's Adam Gillette?" I asked.

"Thomas's arch-rival," Ross said.

That didn't sound right. "If this Adam Gillette is such a big deal, how come I've never heard of him?"

Eric's eyes flashed with interest. "You follow sports?"

"I read the paper," I said.

Now Ross looked pleased, too.

"Relax, guys," I said. "I'm new here, remember? When you're new, you have to make an extra effort to find out what's what and who's who. I don't remember reading anything about this Adam Gillette."

"That's because Eric wrote his final article about Adam last winter. It was an obituary."

"Bad tackle on the football field?" I asked. You heard about stuff like that happening all the time — a promising young athlete plays too hard and all of a sudden it's game over.

"Stupid accident," Eric said. "He fell through the

ice on the lake and drowned."

"City kids," Ross said, shaking his head. "All they know is skating rinks. They think ice is ice and don't know a thing about safety when it comes to the real deal."

Eric hit the Save button on his keyboard, then leaned back in his chair.

"Adam was hot stuff on the football field," he said, "but he didn't know a thing about natural ice. He went out too far just after a thaw and fell through. Someone saw him and called 9-1-1, but it was too late. And too bad. He was a nice guy. He also kept things interesting around here. Kept Thomas on his toes."

"He outshone Thomas, if you ask me," Ross said. "Anyway, the last thing this newspaper needs is more ink on Thomas Rennie. You'll have to come up with something else, Chloe."

But what?

In the end, I interviewed the president and the membership of the school environmental club — which didn't take long, since they were the same person. My slant: High school students are far too apathetic about safeguarding the earth they will one day inherit. The club president had a look of surprise on his face the whole time he was answering my questions. I got the impression he'd never been paid so much attention before. I don't think he caught on to the fact that I spent most of the interview wondering what I should wear when I went out with Thomas that night.

# Chapter 5

I heard Thomas's car pull up in front of the house. I heard the engine idle for a moment, then die. I waited in the front hall, counting slowly, eight . . . nine . . . ten . . . as I imagined Thomas loping up the driveway and climbing the front steps two at a time. Thirteen . . . fourteen . . . The doorbell rang. Seventeen . . . eighteen . . . nineteen . . . twenty. I know this is going to sound like I not only read those goofy teen magazines, but that I actually take their advice seriously, which, honestly, I don't — not the former, not the latter. But I waited and I counted again. Twenty-one . . . twenty-two . . . twenty-three . . . before I walked the three short steps to the front door and opened it. You don't want to seem overly eager, right? It never pays.

Thomas had a vaguely worried look on his face when I peeked through the window at him. Then he saw me and he smiled, suddenly all confidence. I opened the door and invited him to step in, which he did. While I grabbed my sweater, he stood in the front hall and strained to look into the living room, then into the kitchen. I didn't have to be a master of deductive logic to figure out what was going on.

"He's not here," I said. I admit it, there was probably some obvious irritation in my voice.

"Who?" Thomas at least had the decency to look

alarmed and even slightly guilty.

"Mr. Chief-of-Police. That's who you're looking for, isn't it?"

The tinge of pink embarrassment in his cheeks was charming.

"It was a big deal around here when your dad took the job," Thomas said. "I heard he solved some big murder cases back in Montreal."

"And you were wondering, right?"

He looked confused. "Huh?"

"You were wondering how come a hot-shot homicide detective like Levesque agreed to come to this hole-in-the-wall place. No offense — "

"No problem," he said, but from the look on his face I guessed he was just being polite. Way to go, Chloe. You really know how to win them over on the first date.

"Look, I'm sorry," I said. "And he's not my father. He's my stepfather. It's taken some getting used to — "

"No, I'm the one who's sorry," Thomas said. "I'm not the jerk you probably think I am — "

"I don't think — "

"I admit to some curiosity. Okay, maybe a lot of curiosity. Give me a break. I've lived here all my life. Not that I plan to be saying that when I'm ninety and toothless. And everyone made such a big deal of the guy. They make him sound like a combination of Sherlock Holmes and Mike Hammer. But that's not why I asked you out. Honest."

He brushed a lock of hair — of cute, unruly hair —

out of his eyes. "What do you say we get out of here?"

What do I say? Bye-bye, house. Hello, Thomas Rennie.

* * *

We had a great night roller-skating. Yes, *chers amis* back home, I said roller-skating, as in, renting a pair of skates and putting your feet into deep, dark, moist places where other, strange feet have been. I actually did that. I did it and I didn't gag. *Au contraire, mes amis.* I delighted in it. Thomas and I skated round and round and talked and laughed, and then the clock struck midnight — okay, so in this particular fairy tale it struck ten-thirty — and suddenly there were Matt Walker and the Empty-Headed Queens.

"Hey, guys," Thomas said, looking not at all surprised. "You know Chloe, right?"

You would have needed some pretty sophisticated scientific equipment to detect any smile that might have appeared on Lise's or Daria's face. Matt was more welcoming. He grinned at me and grinned even more enthusiastically at the front of my sweater. Nice guy.

"We were just going to get something to eat," Matt said. "You want to come?"

Thomas looked at me, as if he needed my permission, which I guess he did, since we were on a date. I wanted to shake my head. I wanted to be alone with him. I didn't want to spend the rest of the night shivering in the frosty presence of Lise and Daria. But those lovely blue eyes of Thomas's were pleading, so what could I do? I nodded. His smile widened.

"Sure," he said to Matt. "Sounds good. Come on."

Back home — I couldn't help it, I was still thinking like a tourist, still comparing everything in East Hastings to what I was used to *where I came from*; the way it was, the way it was *supposed* to be. Back home, we would have gone someplace where they served cappuccino or mochaccino or frappaccino, somewhere where the coffee had a name like Sulawesi or Aruban, somewhere where "regular" didn't exist, where it was tall or grande or venti. Well, guess what? They didn't have a place like that in East Hastings. Instead, we ended up at Stella's Great Home Cooking, which was no problem, really. When in Rome, and so on. Except that I ended up sitting across from Thomas in the booth instead of beside him, and the girls were on one side and the boys on the other, which meant that I was squished in beside Lise and Daria.

Thomas ordered a burger and fries. Matt ordered a burger, fries and a shake. Daria wanted diet Coke. Ditto Lise. I asked for a cappuccino and, in return, got a blank look from a tired and bored-looking waitress whose name tag read Gladys.

"We don't have that," she said.

"No cappuccino machine?"

She shook her head.

I sighed. "Just give me a coffee," I said.

She glanced at her watch. "Sanka, right?"

"No," I told her. The whole point of coffee is caffeine. "I want the real deal."

She gave me a look of disapproval that would have been hard enough to take from my mother. From a stranger, well, I pretty much decided then and there, no tip for you, Gladys.

"So, your dad's head cop," Matt said while we waited for our food and drink to arrive. He was still fixated on the front of my sweater.

"My *step*father," I said. I like Levesque. I really do. There's something solid about him, something reliable. But even if he stayed married to Mom for the rest of his natural days, I knew I would never call him Dad. Come on. My name is Chloe Yan. The part of me that doesn't look like my mother looks Chinese. My father was a Chinese medical student who hadn't meant to fall in love, sure hadn't meant to get anyone pregnant, and, once the big accident that was me had happened, had decided to bail out of the marriage. But he was still my father.

"I read you loud and clear," Matt said. Gladys reappeared and slid the food in front of the guys, the drinks in front of the girls.

"Matt has a stepfather, too," Thomas said.

"A step-down-father, if you ask me," Matt said.

"In case you aren't reading the signals," Thomas said, "Matt doesn't like his stepfather."

"Art the Fart," Matt said. "Mr. Huckster."

"Artie's a real estate developer," Thomas said.

"Artie's a jerk," Matt shot back. "I still can't believe she married him."

"Love is strange," Thomas said.

"Love sucks," Lise said. Everyone stared at her. "Well, it does," she said. Then, "I can't believe that woman had the nerve to show her face around here."

What woman? I wondered.

"She and Peter's mom are . . . were . . . are good friends," Thomas said. Then, to me, "We're talking about Eileen Braden. She was at the funeral . . . "

The woman in the navy blue suit, I realized.

"I saw her yesterday," Matt said. "I guess she decided to stick around for a few days. Hey, did she call your dad, Lise? When are they planning to get together?"

"Shut up," Lise said. She gave me a look that was pure venom, even though I hadn't said a word.

"Relax," Matt said. "What's your problem? If you ask me, your dad got lucky with Eileen. My mom just got stupid with Artie."

"She was a good teacher," Thomas said, and took a bite of his burger. I supposed he was talking about Eileen Braden, not Matt's mother.

"Pretty, too," Matt said. "I used to wish I was in her class so I could look at her legs all day. She still has great legs, doesn't she, Thomas?"

Thomas grinned and nodded.

Matt suddenly let out a howl. He bent over. His arm was doing something under the table. Rubbing his shin, I realized. Lise must have kicked him. Now she was shoving Daria out of the booth. Then they were both on their feet.

"Hey," Matt said. "Hey, where are you going?"

Lise didn't answer. She and Daria marched double-time to the ladies' room at the back of Stella's.

"I'm going to have one heck of a bruise," Matt said, rubbing his shin again. "And I'm going to spend the rest of the weekend begging her forgiveness."

Thomas shook his head. "You know how she feels about Eileen Braden," he said. "Didn't it even cross your mind to steer clear of the subject?"

"It crossed my mind," Matt said, "but, hey, I gotta be me." He flashed me a mega-watt smile. "You gotta be true to yourself, right?"

"Sometimes you have to be smart," I told him. Thomas laughed.

"That'll be the day," Thomas said.

"So what's the deal with this Eileen Braden?" I asked. "Why doesn't Lise like her?"

"It's a long story," Matt said.

I glanced back to the door to the ladies' room. If Lise really was angry, she would probably stay in there for a while.

Matt shrugged. "Lise's parents split a few years back. Lise is still mad about it."

"Did one of them fall in love with someone else?" I asked.

Matt shook his head. "It was an age-difference thing. Lise's mother was only eighteen when she married. Lise's dad was in his mid-thirties. From what I heard, Cheri got restless."

"Cheri?"

"Lise's mother," Thomas said. "I heard she got bored in this town."

"Whatever," Matt said. "She took off for France with a girlfriend of hers. It was supposed to be a vacation. It ended up being a permanent change of residence. Lise took it pretty hard. So did her dad — until he started dating Eileen Braden."

"Lise took that hard, too," Thomas said.

"She kept hoping her mom would come home and her parents would get back together. Obviously, if her dad got serious about Eileen, Lise's hopes would be toast," Matt said.

"Fortunately for Lise — " Thomas began.

"And unfortunately for Paul Arsenault, Lise's father — " Matt chimed in.

"Old Paul turned out to be the jealous type."

"Or," Thomas said, "old Eileen turned out to be the play-the-field type."

I laughed. They were like a couple of old gossips. Not exactly what you expect in the high school football team's starting line.

"Tell me everything," I said, playing gossip along with them.

"Eileen Braden played bridge competitively," Matt said. "Her partner was another teacher from school, a male teacher. Paul didn't like that. He tried to make her find another partner. She refused. Then he tried to make her quit. She refused. Lise says it was the only thing they ever fought about. Then the guy Eileen played with — "

" — played *bridge* with," Thomas said.

"Well, maybe they only played bridge together and maybe they played something else," Matt said. "I guess Paul thinks their friendship went beyond bridge. The guy sent her flowers, after all. Do bridge partners send each other flowers?"

Thomas shrugged. So did I. Who understood bridge, let alone bridge players?

"Anyway," Matt said, "the lovebirds eventually broke up and Eileen Braden moved to Morrisville." Morrisville was about eighty miles north of East Hastings.

"So if it's over, why does Lise still hate Eileen?" I asked.

Matt shrugged. "All I know is that Lise's mother is supposed to come back for a visit at Christmas and Lise is still hoping for a reunion — which isn't likely to happen if her dad gets involved with Eileen again."

I glanced past his shoulder and saw Lise and Daria coming out of the ladies' room. Matt followed my look. He got up and hurried back to meet Lise. She brushed past him. He followed her like a well-trained puppy. Thomas was right: Love is strange. Lise didn't stop at the booth. She walked right by, with Matt on her heels. Daria hesitated, as if she wasn't sure what to do, go with Lise and Matt, or stay with me and Thomas. She chose neither.

"I'm going home," she announced, and headed for the door alone.

Instead of being perturbed about being abandoned by his friends, Thomas seemed pleased.

"Alone at last," he said. He grinned while he munched on the rest of his burger.

I was pleased, too, until I glanced at the clock on the wall.

"I have to go," I said. Mom had always been strict about curfews. Now she had Levesque to back her up. It wasn't worth the effort to take on the two of them. I would never win. Thomas looked disappointed, but seemed to understand.

* * *

They were waiting up for me, of course. They always waited up.

"Sorry," I said. Parents, step or otherwise, love to hear that word. Come in waving the white flag of surrender and seven times out of ten, they'll let it go at that. "I lost track of the time. Besides, I'm only twenty minutes late. I'm sorry, it won't happen again, really."

"It's okay," Mom said. She hugged me. Hmmm. Something was up. "Mrs. Flosnick was here this evening," she said. Double-hmmm. "She wanted to talk to you."

"Me?" Why would Mrs. Flosnick want to talk to me?

"She wanted to ask you a favor."

"What kind of favor?"

"The school called her about Peter's personal effects. You know, the things in his locker and in the newspaper office. Mrs. Flosnick was wondering if you would mind collecting them for her and taking them to her house."

"Me?"

"She says Peter never liked people to go through his things. He was very private. But she didn't think he would have minded if you did it since you and he were friends."

Wait a minute!

Levesque was giving me a peculiar look.

"We weren't friends, Mom," I said. "I hardly knew the guy."

My mother didn't argue with me. "Peter's mother is going through a difficult time, Chloe. Peter was an only child and Mrs. Flosnick was widowed when he was small. He was all she had. Peter didn't have a lot of friends, but if Mrs. Flosnick wants to believe that he did, what's the harm?"

I remembered Mrs. Flosnick on our front porch, crying one minute, defending her son the next. Mom was right. What was the harm?

"When does she want me to do it?"

"She didn't say. I guess the sooner the better. You might as well get it over with, both her and you." She hesitated a moment. "I know it wasn't my place, but I told her I didn't think you'd mind."

I nodded. "Okay," I said. "I'll do it."

# Chapter 6

"Hi," Thomas said. One word. One syllable, and honestly, it rocked my world. It made me remember Friday night when he pulled his ten-year-old Mustang up in front of the house and killed the engine. He had looked up at my house and then he looked at me with the same look you'd give a great novel after you'd just read the last page, the same look you'd give the Montreal Forum after a concert you didn't want to end, the same look you'd give a plate that had been heaped with the best meal you'd ever eaten just after you'd swallowed the last mouthful.

Okay, so maybe that was the look I gave *him* and maybe the one he gave me was just goodnight. Don't think I didn't lie awake half the night wondering which was which. And don't think I didn't spend the better part of the weekend jumping every time the phone rang and wishing I believed what my mother always said, that in this day and age it was okay for a girl to call a guy the day after that all-important first date.

People have said that I'm stubborn. Maybe that's why I didn't call Thomas on Saturday or on Sunday, even though he was on my mind every second of every minute of both days. He had taken the first step, after all, and he knew where to find me.

If — when? — he decided that he hadn't made the biggest mistake of his life when he'd asked me out, he could call me.

He didn't.

And then, no sooner had I stepped onto school property on Monday morning than there he was, waving to me, hurrying across the parking lot toward me, smiling, saying, "Hi," making my heart race like a well-tuned engine.

My, "Hi," in return probably sounded frosty. He hadn't phoned all weekend. What was I supposed to make of that?

"I was going to call you," he said. I braced myself. Here they come, the infamous lame excuses. *I was going to call you, but the dog ate my phone book. I was going to call you, but our house burned down and your phone number went up in flames along with all the family heirlooms. I was going to call you . . .*

" — but to tell you the truth, I was afraid to."

A ten-point bonus for originality . . . and a possible twenty-five point penalty for offensive behavior. What was I, some kind of dragon lady? What was there to be afraid of?

"Excuse me?" I said.

"Not of you," he said quickly. "I wasn't afraid of you. But . . . " He looked down at his feet for a second or two. "Your stepdad looks like the kind of guy who's real comfortable with the idea of giving people the third degree. I . . . " Now he looked sheepish. "I kept imagining him answering the phone."

He dropped his voice down low in a fair approximation of Levesque's. "Chloe? Why do you want to talk to Chloe, young man? What did you say your name was? What are your intentions with regard to her?"

Good question.

"He's not *that* scary," I said, even though sometimes he was. Big and scary.

Thomas slumped. Well, why not? I had practically accused him of being a coward.

"I really enjoyed Friday night," he said.

"So did I."

He looked directly at me with those sweet blue eyes of his. "You did?"

"Sure."

Now he smiled, shyly, which turned out to be charming.

"You want to do something after school?" he said. "We could go for coffee and talk. We could take a long walk in the park. There's a great trail that follows the lake."

"I can't." I could have said, I'm sorry, I can't. I could have said, I'd love to, but I can't. I didn't. Then I saw disappointment in his face — it looked like genuine disappointment — and I wished that I had been a little nicer. "I promised to do something after school," I said. I could practically read his mind (Did you promise to do something with another guy?) and decided to put him out of his misery. "I promised Mrs. Flosnick I'd clean out Peter's locker for her."

Now he looked baffled. "Hey, were you and Flosnick — "

"I barely knew the guy. But his mother has this idea that we were best buddies."

Thomas chuckled. "Sounds like maybe you had a secret admirer," he said.

I'm glad someone found that amusing. "Look, his mother asked my mother to ask me if I would bring his stuff home for her. She's having a tough time. He was her only child and she's a widow — "

"Whoa," Thomas said. "It's okay. I was kidding."

Yeah, right. He was enjoying the idea that the geekiest guy in school had selected me as the object of his affection.

"Why don't I give you a hand?" Thomas said. "I'll meet you after school and we'll take care of it together. Okay?"

"You mean it?"

He nodded.

"Okay."

* * *

We had to go to the school office to get someone to open Peter's locker for us. Ms. Jeffries shook her head. "We would have been happy to take care of this for Mrs. Flosnick," she said. Still, she got Mr. Luckhardt, a.k.a. Mr. Maintenance, to open Peter's locker for us. Mr. Luckhardt gave us two cardboard boxes.

"School textbooks in one, which you can hand in at the office," he said. "Personal belongings in the other."

If you were to empty my locker of everything that belonged to the school, you wouldn't be left with much else: a pile of notebooks, the small mirror that hangs inside the door so I can check my makeup and my hair, a dollar-store umbrella (just in case), a sweater (ditto), a dried-out tube of mascara I should have thrown out weeks ago. Peter's locker was something else. After Thomas had picked out all the textbooks, which were mostly on the top shelf, there was still tons more stuff to sort through.

Thomas held up one of a stack of notebooks. "Can't we just pitch these?" he asked.

I shook my head. "We should let Mrs. Flosnick decide what she wants to keep and what she wants to toss." A thick stack of science and astronomy magazines, another stack of paperbacks, mostly science fiction, but a few mysteries as well, and the Edgar Allan Poe short story collection that had narrowly missed my head a few days before Peter died. A camera. "Any film in it?" Thomas asked. I checked. "Nope." A tape recorder, with no tape in it — I checked. "The guy was always talking into that thing," Thomas said, "like it was his best friend." A pair of sneakers, an old T-shirt and five — count 'em, five — moldy gym socks. He dropped these last items into the "keeper" box. "I can see where Mrs. F. would want to hang on to these. They pretty much sum up the guy." I took out the socks and threw them in the garbage.

"Can you manage that?" I asked as he hoisted the box.

"Sure," he said. "I'm an athlete, remember?"

I laughed. "Good. Next stop, the newspaper office."

"I thought the next stop was my car."

"It is, *after* the newspaper office."

"Guess that'll teach me to volunteer." But he smiled and, like an obedient servant, followed me down to the basement.

Ross Jenkins looked pleased when he saw me enter the office. He looked less pleased when he saw that Thomas was with me.

"Second desk from the window, top drawer," Ross said, when I told him why we were here. "If his mother wants everything, I guess you'd better empty his mail slot, too."

"Mail slot?"

Ross nodded to the far wall, where a set of shelves was attached to the wall. I'd forgotten about the mail slots.

"Peter's is always full," he said. "Either the guy gets more mail than Santa Claus at Christmas, or he's really bad — uh, *was* really bad — at emptying his mail."

"We're going to need another box," Thomas said from the second desk from the window. He had already opened Peter's drawer and was peering down into it. From where I was standing, I could see it was crammed with papers.

Ross stared at Thomas, then at me. Then he shook his head.

"Figures," he muttered.

"What figures?" I asked.

"Nothing," Ross said. He hook his head again. "I think I have a couple of boxes in my office. I'll take a look."

I joined Thomas and started pulling things out of the deep drawer. Almost everything had something to do with either space or astronomy: astronomy magazines; a bundle of newspaper clippings about the Pathfinder probe to Mars, the Hubble telescope, the failing Mir space station; three different star maps; a stack of photographs of the night sky, taken, I guess, by Peter; a sheaf of letters about stars and astronomy addressed to Peter by members of high school astronomy clubs all over the province. Ross found a box in his office and brought it to me.

"Pack this stuff, will you?" I said to Thomas. I went over to the mail slots, located Peter's, which was stuffed full of magazines and all kinds of envelopes — big, small, fat and thick — and carried everything back to where Thomas was. "I guess that's everything," I said. "Most of this stuff hasn't even been opened. You sure you want me to give it to Mrs. Flosnick?"

"What would we do with it here?" Ross said. "If it's addressed to Peter, then it's his property. Besides, it's not like anyone else in this school is going to step forward and take over his astronomy column. I don't think there's a single person in this whole region, with the exception of some professors in the science department at the university, who knows as much about the subject as Peter did."

I supposed he was right. I dumped the unopened, unread magazines and correspondence into the box that Thomas was filling with opened and presumably read magazines and correspondence.

"I guess that's everything," I said at last.

"It's about time," Thomas said.

He carried the heavier box filled with the things we had emptied from Peter's locker. I carried the newspaper stuff. We put both boxes in the trunk of his car and drove to Mrs. Flosnick's.

"Where would you like us to put these?" I asked when she answered the door.

"Up in his room, I suppose," Mrs. Flosnick said. She was staring at the boxes as if they were filled with spiders and snakes, which, I guess, is exactly what memories can be to some people. It wasn't hard to imagine her picking through the boxes after we left, reading his notes and letters, flipping through his books and magazines, remembering how much he liked science, how passionate he was about what he saw up in the sky at night. "It's right at the top of the stairs."

Peter's room was twice as big as mine. The shelves that lined one wall were filled with books, mostly science and science fiction, and magazines, mostly science and astronomy. Another wall was papered with posters and photographs of stars and planets. On a table beside his bed was a videocamera and a regular camera that looked more expensive than the one we had found in his locker. So did the large telescope that stood in front of the window. That part-time job of Peter's at the flower shop must have really pulled in the bucks. I set down the box I was holding, crossed to the window, and peered through the telescope's eyepiece. Well, tried to peer. The eyepiece was awkward and not at all comfortable. It didn't have one of those rubber-rimmed ends that most telescopes have so that you can press your eye up against it. I pulled back and examined the thing. An odd, round metal frame had been attached over the rubbery part. But why? I bent to the telescope again and, more carefully this time, looked through the eyepiece.

"Wow," I said. "This is really something! I can actually see into the windows of that housing development over there."

Thomas came to where I was standing and peeked out the window.

"Artieville," he said.

"What?"

"Artieville. That's what Matt calls it. A couple of years ago, that subdivision was a meadow. From here you would have had a clear view of the lake. Then Artie Lambton — you know, Art the Fart, Matt's stepfather — bought the land and turned it into East Hastings' new suburbia, which a lot of people would argue we didn't need, seeing as how we barely have an *urbia*. Where do you want me to put this?"

*This* was the box he was still holding.

"On the desk, I guess," I said. I peered through

the telescope again. The thing must have cost a fortune. But if that was so, why was the eyepiece so strange? Why didn't it allow for more comfortable viewing?

"Peter loved that telescope more than anything else in the world," a voice said from the door. Mrs. Flosnick's voice. She startled me. I hadn't realized she was standing there, and I felt like an intruder using Peter's things without having been invited. I straightened up in a hurry, knocking against the desk as I did so. The box Thomas has set on it shifted and looked like it was going to topple over. I caught it just in time — well, almost just in time. A couple of books cascaded to the floor.

"He spent hours staring through that telescope," Mrs. Flosnick said. "He even attached a videocamera to the lens so that he could videotape the movement of the stars." She smiled. "I watched one of those tapes once. To tell you the truth, I didn't see any movement at all. But Peter did, night to night, month to month. He shot hours of tape." She pointed to a place on the bookshelf that was packed with black plastic video covers. "Sometimes he'd sit up here and watch them, all fourteen of them. That's one hundred and twelve hours in total. I know because he told me. To me, it looked about as exciting as watching grass grow, but Peter loved watching them. He said he found it relaxing. He said every time he watched one of those tapes, he saw something he hadn't noticed the time before." Her smile slipped into a quivery, close-to-tears sigh. "I know a lot of people thought he was a little odd. But I'll bet Albert Einstein was an odd little boy, don't you think? And what about Carl Sagan? I heard he always loved the stars, and look what he made of his life."

I stopped to retrieve the books I had knocked over. One of them was the Edgar Allan Poe book. A slip of paper was sticking out from it. It looked like a receipt of some kind. I looked at it more closely. It was a receipt from the flower shop where Peter used to work. He was probably using it as a bookmark. I tucked it back into the book and set it back on top of the box it had fallen from.

"We'd better be going," I said. "If there's ever anything else I can do, Mrs. Flosnick . . . " I hoped there wasn't, but you have to be polite, right?

"You've done so much already," she said.

I hadn't actually done a thing. I was beginning to wish I had. I was beginning to wish I had said hi to Peter at least once, or maybe even had a conversation with him so that I could honestly say something nice about him, something that would make his mother feel a little better. But I hadn't, and I couldn't. There was nothing to do now but follow Thomas down the stairs and out the door.

# Chapter 7

Daria Dattillo may have been uncomfortable with the publicity or notoriety, however limited, that came with being interviewed for a high school newspaper, but she apparently didn't mind the publicity or notoriety that came with having her poems published in the same newspaper. To my surprise, there were four of them on page three. I looked at them, then at Ross.

"Since when are you editor of a literary journal?" I said.

"Since when are you captain of the cheerleading squad?" he muttered.

At least, I think that's what he muttered. "Excuse me?"

"Nothing." He didn't smile at me, which was a first.

"What's going on, Ross?" I asked.

"Nothing."

"How come there are poems on page three?"

"Ask Ms. Peters."

"I'm asking you."

He flung down the copy of the newspaper he had been holding. "It wasn't my idea," he said. "I told Ms. Peters that we have a literary journal here at school that has a *mandate* — " he gave a nasty twist to the word " — to publish fiction and poetry, whereas the newspaper *mandate* is to publish news. I told her that poetry isn't news and that it doesn't belong in the newspaper. But she disagreed. She said that Daria's poetry is news, especially since she won that stupid poetry contest. She also pointed out that there was more than enough space to run the poems because *someone* didn't complete her profile assignment — "

"Hey, don't blame me," I shot back. "I tried to get that profile done. Daria refused to cooperate and then Ms. Peters told me to back off."

"And I suppose if you were a Washington reporter and you had been told to back off the Lewinsky story, you would have obeyed, right?"

He sounded bitter.

"Daria Dattillo's prize-winning poem isn't exactly Lewinsky," I yelled at him. "Look, I don't know what your problem is, Ross. I tried to do the profile. You know I did. I didn't ask for that assignment. I don't care about her stupid poems. What's more, I don't think anyone in the whole school cares about her stupid poems — with the possible exception of Ms. Peters." Suddenly I had that weird, wonderful feeling you get when you finally solve a nearly impossible puzzle. "Oh . . . I get it." I couldn't help it. I grinned. "You're jealous."

"I am not," Ross said. His face said something completely different.

"You're jealous because ever since Daria won that contest, Ms. Peters has been making a big fuss over her. And if she's making a big fuss over Daria, she's not making a big fuss over you. Admit it, Ross, you're angry because you feel shut out."

"I do not," he said. But his shoulders sagged, and he slumped down into a chair. "Okay, so maybe that's part of it. But, come on, poetry in the newspaper? When was the last time you opened the morning paper and saw a wad of poems on page three? Ms. Peters is going overboard. She's completely rewritten the mandate of the newspaper just so Daria can get bigger exposure. That's not right."

"So, tell her."

"I did."

"And?"

"I already told you what she said. What could I do?"

I think he wanted me to commiserate with him. I think he wanted me to tell him that Ms. Peters was wrong, that she had used her advisor status inappropriately, and — oh yes — poor, poor Ross.

"You should have stuck to your guns," I said instead.

His sulky expression was replaced by one of pure surprise. "What?"

"You should have stuck to your guns. You're always making a big deal about journalistic ethics and integrity. If you think she was wrong, you should have stood your ground."

"She would have — " he began, then broke off abruptly.

"She would have what? Fired you as editor? No,

she wouldn't. And what if she had? Wouldn't you rather take a stand on principle than get backed into doing something you think is wrong? Wouldn't you rather dissociate yourself completely from something you disapprove of so strongly than have to spend the rest of the day, maybe the rest of the week, telling people that it wasn't your fault? You're supposed to be the editor. What kind of editor lets things appear in his newspaper that he doesn't think are news? Unless maybe it's an editor who doesn't want his advisor to get mad at him."

Ross's face got redder and redder as I talked, so I knew I had struck a nerve. When I had finished he got up, said, "Thank you so much for your support," and marched out of the newspaper office.

"You're welcome," I said to the door as it closed behind him.

After Ross had gone, I sat down at my desk and opened the newspaper again. I'm not anti-culture. In fact, I read a lot. I treasure my library card because there's no way I could ever have afforded to buy all the books I've read. I'm not anti-poetry, either. I haven't read volumes of it, but I have read some. I've enjoyed some, too. But, I'm sorry, is there a sixteen-year-old alive (or dead, for that matter) who ever managed to write a *great* poem? And what are the chances that, should such a creature magically appear on this planet, he/she would end up in East Hastings and be published in the East Hastings Regional High newspaper? Still, a mature mind is an open mind — I had a teacher once who said that ad nauseam. Little kids every-where refuse to eat new dishes by saying, "I don't like it." Mothers everywhere respond by saying, "How do you know you don't like it when you haven't even tried it?" Moral of the story: You can't make up your mind you don't like something with-out at least giving it a chance. I sat in my chair at my desk (well, my desk for the moment — if Eric Moore were to show up, he'd probably make the same claim) and I read the Daria Dattillo poems that had been printed on page three.

They were okay, but I wasn't wild about them. There was something else about them, something that bothered me, but I couldn't quite figure out what or why.

I dumped the paper and turned my thoughts to a personal viewpoint story I had decided to write — a non-sports-fan's view of high school athletes. It was beginning to interest me how so many girls — and I could now count myself among them — didn't really like sports but adored high school sports stars. A big bonus: This would give me an excuse to interview Thomas. So much for *my* journalistic ethics.

\* \* \*

I saw Lise Arsenault out of the corner of my eye. Saw her, but registered nothing. I was sitting on the bleachers that ran along one side of the football field, enjoying the fresh air, the blue sky, the quiet and the few minutes of freedom I had left before classes started again for the afternoon. I was also kind of hoping that I might run into Thomas, too.

Instead, there was Lise. I thought of tossing her a wave, but decided against it. Waving would just give her the opportunity to ignore me. So I glanced at her, then looked back down at the book I had been reading. I didn't look up again until a shadow fell across my page. Lise's shadow.

I opened my mouth to say hi, then closed it again. Let *her* make the first move.

"Are you going out with Thomas or what?" she said. That's "said" as in demanded.

Fine, thank you, and how are you, Lise? "Excuse me?" I said.

"I said, are you going out with Thomas?"

"I'm sorry," I said, "but I don't see what that has to do with you." Oh, and by the way, that look you're giving me, the one that makes it clear that you think I'm the word that rhymes with rich, that's not going to help you pry an answer out of me.

"If you're going out with Thomas, I have a right to know."

"Really?" I asked. She was getting on my nerves now. Nobody, not even my mother — well, maybe my mother, but no one else — could use that tone on me and get away with it. "What are you, the boyfriend monitor?"

Her face seemed to be fighting with itself. She started to scowl, then appeared to think better of it. While she didn't exactly smile, she did drop down onto the bleachers beside me.

"Thomas is best friends with Matt, and I'm going

out with Matt."

Now tell me something I don't know. "And?"

"Daria is my best friend."

Uh-huh. "And?" I was having a little trouble understanding what she was getting at. "Until you came along, Matt and me and Thomas and Daria were a foursome."

"Thomas was going out with Daria?" This was news to me.

"Did I say that?" There was that tone again, the one that made me want to get up and walk away, which is exactly what I started to do. "I'm sorry," Lise said. "What I mean is, we've been hanging around together and now if Thomas is going out with you, it puts Daria in an awkward position."

"In what way?"

"She's a fifth."

"A fifth?"

"A fifth person. Matt and me are a pair." A pair of what? I wanted to ask. "If you're going out with Thomas, that makes you and him a pair. And that leaves Daria."

"Let me get this straight," I said slowly. "You want me to stop seeing Thomas so that Daria, who isn't seeing Thomas, can be a fourth, not a fifth. Is that it?"

"I didn't say that."

"What then?"

"I just think I have a right to know, that's all. So does Daria."

"Fine," I said. "Now you do."

She stood up as abruptly as she had sat down.

"I used to go out with Thomas," she said. "I still feel protective of him."

"Oh." I supposed — just barely — that it was possible Lise could care about someone other than herself.

"He's a nice guy," she said, "and a good person. He had a really rough time last winter and he's only just getting over it. I don't want to see him messed up again."

There were a few things I could have said. I could have said, thanks for the vote of confidence, Lise. I could have said, whoa, you must be clairvoyant because, yup, that's just want I was planning to do, I was planning to mess the guy up. Instead, I decided to take the high road.

"What do you mean, a rough time?"

"A guy he was close to died accidentally."

"You mean Adam Gillette?"

She looked surprised.

"I share a desk in the newspaper office with Eric Moore," I said.

She nodded. "Thomas and Adam were friends."

"I heard they were rivals."

She smiled, one of those sad little smiles. "They were. On the football field, off the football field, those two went at it all the time. But Thomas really liked Adam. He admired him, you know? Thomas was the star of the football team — he'd been the star of every team he was on since back in first grade. It was always so easy for him. Then

Adam came along." She smiled again, and shook her head. "Adam made everything harder for Thomas. If Thomas screwed up or if he got lazy, there was Adam, ready to grab the glory. I think Thomas got a real kick out of that. It made everything more exciting. I used to think that without Adam there snapping at his heels, life would have been boring for Thomas. He took it really hard when Adam died. And I mean really hard. He couldn't concentrate, he was so moody his grades dropped. If he hadn't had his heart set on that football scholarship, he probably would have started screwing up on the football field too." No more smiles now. What did I see glistening in her eyes? Not tears. Please not tears. The last thing I wanted to know was that she was still carrying a torch for Thomas.

"We broke up about two months after Adam died," she said. "And it's only recently that Thomas has started to snap out of it. I don't want anything to go wrong for him again. Okay?"

What could I say? "Okay."

* * *

Schoolwork plants the seed of knowledge. Homework makes it take root. Mr. Stevenson, my grade seven teacher, used to say that when he was writing our homework assignments on the blackboard. I hated him for it. But I knew he was right and, in the past year, I had started to take my homework seriously. There was going to be no Wal-Mart in my future if I could help it.

So there I was that evening, in my room, history textbook open on my lap. I was supposed to be studying for a history quiz, but instead I was thinking about what Lise had told me. I was thinking, too, about what you think when you meet someone for the first or even second time and about how wrong you could be about them. Thomas seemed like the kind of guy who liked to have fun, not the kind of guy who would ever become depressed. He was a jock, and, sure, I liked him a lot, but it hadn't occurred to me that there had been tragedy in his life and that he had had trouble dealing with it. Maybe he would have told me about it eventually. Or maybe I should be grateful to Lise for giving me that insight. Either way, I kept trying to imagine how I would feel if someone I knew and liked and, if Lise was right, admired, suddenly died. Nothing like that had ever happened to me.

# Chapter 8

There's good timing and then there's dropping in on someone when they're in the middle of a screaming match with their stepfather. Of course, it didn't help that Matt and his stepfather Artie Lambton were screaming at each other in the middle of their front lawn.

"Maybe this isn't a good time to interrupt," I suggested to Thomas.

Thomas just shrugged and put his car in Park.

"When it comes to those two, there's never a good time," he said. "Besides, I promised to pick up Matt." He reached for the door handle.

"You're not going out there while they're still arguing, are you?" I said.

"Why not? They're mad at each other, not at me."

"Maybe they want their privacy."

Thomas laughed. "They're in their front yard, Chloe. If they wanted privacy, they'd be shouting at each other inside the house, not outside."

He opened the car door and was about to get out when a woman appeared on the porch. A slender woman with big, sad eyes. Thomas settled back in his seat. Matt and his stepfather turned toward the woman.

"Lenore," Thomas said.

"Huh?"

86

"That's Matt's mother, Lenore."

Lenore Walker Lambton kissed her husband lightly on the cheek, then took her son by the hand. Matt started to pull away from her, but Lenore held tight, and, from where I was sitting, it didn't look like Matt was struggling hard to break free. He let her hold on. He seemed to listen to what she was saying. Listen, but not agree. He shook his head. Lenore glanced at Artie, who threw up his hands and turned away. Then she said something to him and he turned back to Matt. I couldn't hear what she was saying, but I could make out one word her lips were forming: "Please." She said it several times until finally Artie thrust out a hand. Matt stared at it as if it were holding a knife or a gun, but he finally grasped it. A blind man could have read the distaste on Matt's face. Thomas tooted the horn on the steering wheel. I glanced at him.

"Everyone saves face, right?" he explained. Sure enough, all three people on the lawn turned to look at us. Lenore's smile was one of relief and gratitude. Artie shook his head, then slipped an arm around Lenore's waist. He smiled at us and waved. Matt ran across the lawn to the car.

"Don't forget your curfew, kiddo," Artie called after him.

Matt winced as he opened the car door and slid into the back seat.

"Creep," he muttered as he slammed the door. Then, to Thomas, "Come on, let's get out of here."

Thomas turned the key in the ignition and off we

went. "Are we picking up Lise?" he asked.

"She's going to meet us at the library," Matt said.

Thomas nodded.

I hadn't thought about it before, but now I wondered how Thomas felt about Matt dating his ex-girlfriend. Did it bother him? It had to be weird to see someone else — especially if that someone was your best friend — holding the hand that you held not so long ago, wrapping his arm around shoulders that you used to wrap your arm around, kissing the cheek that you once brushed your lips against. I know I would have found it hard to take. But then again, East Hastings was a small town and while it wasn't exactly accurate to say that everyone knew everyone else, the dating pool was limited. Maybe things like this happened all the time.

Lise was pacing up and down on the sidewalk outside the library. She was alone — something that surprised me. I had gotten used to seeing her as part of a pair, Lise-and-Daria. She turned when she saw Thomas's car and hurried toward it.

"What took you guys so long?" she asked as we all piled out into the parking lot. "I've been standing out here for fifteen minutes."

"Trouble in Artieville," Thomas said.

She looked at Matt, her blue eyes little puddles of concern.

"It's no big deal," Matt said. "He was giving me grief over the school thing again, that's all."

What school thing? I wondered. But I knew my

limitations as an outsider. I didn't ask.

"It's none of his business," Lise said. "It's up to your mother, not him."

"He influences her," Matt said. "He influences her and she lets him. She was never like that with Dad. With Dad, she was more of a partner. But she does what Artie tells her, and Artie has convinced her that I have to do it on my own or else."

Do what on his own? I wondered. Or else what?

"Too bad those rumors didn't turn out to be true, huh?" Thomas said. "Life would have been different."

Rumors? What rumors?

We had reached the front door to the library. Conversation died temporarily as we pushed our way through the turnstiles, climbed up to the second floor and scouted out some empty seats. Lise and Matt claimed a table tucked away in the back of the stacks. Thomas headed for one near the window, and sat so that he could overlook the street.

"I like to have a view when I study," he said.

"The only view you're supposed to have is a view of your books."

He grinned.

"What?" I asked.

"What?"

"What's that look?"

"What look?"

"You know what I mean."

His grin widened. "You sound just like my parents."

Ouch.

"We have midterms in two weeks," I said. "We're supposed to be studying. That's why we're here, remember?"

He shrugged. "No sweat," he said. "I'm doing okay."

"But if you want to go to university . . . " There was that grin again. "What?"

"What?"

"You're giving me that look again."

He slipped an arm around my shoulder. It wasn't the first time a guy had done that, but it sure felt nice. It felt cozy.

"I'm going to study," he said. "But I practically have a scholarship in the bag. Unless I take a bad tackle and break my neck or something, which isn't likely, I have nothing to worry about."

"*You* have a scholarship?" Okay, so maybe I sounded more surprised than was diplomatic.

"I've been scouted by a couple of American schools," he said. "I've been offered a football scholarship."

Some guys have all the luck.

"You should still study," I said. It sounded lame, and I knew it.

"I am studying. I'm studying your face."

Uh-huh. "Geez, Thomas, I haven't heard that one since I housebroke my dinosaur."

He laughed, but didn't take his arm away. I was glad. And I have to admit, I was reluctant to end such a fine moment by hauling out my history text.

"So what's the deal with Matt's stepfather?" I asked.

Thomas slid his chair closer to me, so that he could hold me more tightly.

"What do you want to know?"

We didn't get much work done that night. Instead we sat close together, his arm around me, his breath warm on my neck, and he filled me in on Matt. His father had died in a plane crash when Matt was nine years old. He had left Matt's mother Lenore in what Thomas called "pretty good shape" financially.

"My dad says Matt's dad was born with a silver spoon in his mouth," Thomas said. "I say if that's true, it's a miracle the kid didn't choke when he drew his first breath."

"Ha, ha."

Until two years ago, Thomas said Matt and his mother had lived alone in a big house near the park. Then Lenore Walker met Artie Lambton.

"She spent most of her time after her husband's death just taking care of Matt," Thomas went on. "I don't think she had much personal life at all. She was home all the time, being mom. At first Matt didn't mind. Then, you know how it is, you get to be a certain age and you don't want your mom focusing her attention on you all the time. So Matt started nagging her to take a class or something. The way he tells it, he had to practically push her out the door to get her to go with a friend of hers to a reading at the bookstore. Some big-deal author she liked was in town. And guess who she met that night?"

"Artie."

Thomas nodded. "As far as I know, Artie's not a big reader. Who knows what he was doing at the reading. Maybe he was out looking for women. Boy, I tell you, Matt sure regrets forcing his mother to go out that night. Somehow she and Artie ended up having coffee together that same night. Then he called her the next day and asked her out for dinner and they saw each other pretty much regularly after that. Last Christmas he proposed and she accepted. Matt's been ticked off ever since."

"He proposed to Matt's *mother,* not Matt," I said. "He should be glad she found someone else."

"Matt's a good guy," Thomas said. "He wants his mother to be happy. He just doesn't want her to be happy with Artie."

"Why not? The guy can't be that bad."

Thomas leaned closer to me. I felt his lips on my cheek.

"You have to promise to keep your mouth shut about this. Matt doesn't like people talking about his mother."

"I promise." If he kissed me on the cheek again, I would promise him the world.

"Matt thinks Artie only married his mother for her money. The guy's a huckster, always talking about making millions of dollars on this deal and that deal. The word is that just before Artie proposed to Lenore, he was up to his eyeballs in debt with the construction of Artieville."

"That's not its real name, is it?"

"Clear Meadows," Thomas said. "He called it Clear Meadows, and it almost did him in. Artie didn't exactly pick the right time to build — things have been pretty slow up here for a couple of years now. By last Christmas almost half of the houses were framed and most of the rest were just being finished, but I don't think Artie had sold more than two or three of them. The word was that he owed money to everyone — contractors, suppliers, laborers, you name it. Everyone was saying that Artie didn't even have the money to insure the development — you know, in case anything went wrong. Then, on Christmas Eve, just when Artie was getting ready to ask Lenore to marry him, Artieville went up in flames. A batch of townhouses burned to the ground, and some other houses were badly smoke-damaged."

"What caused it?"

"Careless smoking, somebody leaving a lit cigarette around — that's what the fire marshal said. Anyway, everyone thought that was the end of the road for Artie, that he'd been wiped out and would have to declare bankruptcy. Matt was practically jumping for joy. I think he thought that the guy would look like such a failure and he'd be so broke, Lenore wouldn't touch him."

"That's not what happened?"

Thomas glanced back toward the stacks where Matt and Lise were hidden and doing who knows what. Then he cuddled up even closer with me.

"Lenore had already bailed Artie out," he said. "She'd become a silent partner in his company. She had paid all his bills, including insurance premiums on the development. Apparently she had taken out the policy months before the fire. The insurance company paid for the damages, Artieville went ahead, most of the places were sold by Easter. Artie made a ton of money. And Artie and Lenore got married."

"Too bad for Matt."

Thomas shrugged. "He'll live. In another couple of years, he'll be out of here. Besides, Lenore is happy. That's important, right? It's not as if Matt was going to stay at home with his mother for the rest of his life."

"True."

* * *

When you're hot (like last night), you're hot. When you're not, you're not. I was definitely not hot the next day. I sat in front of my computer in the newspaper office, a can of pop at my elbow, a deadline staring me in the face, and I couldn't write a word.

Maybe it was because I was too happy. So happy that I had barely slept the night before. Instead, I had tossed and turned in my bed, tangling myself up in the sheets, thinking about Thomas, seeing his face, feeling his hand on my shoulder.

Or maybe it was because I was too annoyed to think after what had happened in English class. Day three on our schedule was creative writing, and this was day three. This week the assigned method of self-expression was poetry. I freely admit that my poem — okay, my *attempt* at a poem, a sonnet, to be precise — wasn't in the same league as, say, Shakespeare. But I had tried. With a few exceptions, everyone in the class had tried. Ms. Peters asked a few of us to read our work aloud, which we did. Her comments on our efforts were brief, to say the least, and far from encouraging. Then she read out a poem that I recognized. I had seen it in the school paper. It was one of Daria's poems. She read it and then another and then, gag, another, and she spent the rest of English class — twenty-five full minutes — explaining why Daria's poems "worked," as she put it, and what we could all learn from Daria's shining example. It really ticked me off, and not because she hadn't praised my poem. I was annoyed because Ms. Peters carried on as if Daria were Dylan Thomas or Sylvia Plath, which, trust me, I know enough to know that she wasn't. I was sick to death of hearing about Daria, and was sicker still of the modest pose Daria always struck when the subject of her poetry came up. She sat in silence, her head bowed, perfectly motionless — oh, look at humble little me — all through class.

No wonder I was suffering from writer's block.

I sat with my hands frozen on the keyboard, the can of pop growing warm, knowing I had to finish my article — I was writing on why I didn't think kids should have to sell chocolate bars in order to pay for musical instruments for the school music program, that's what our parents pay taxes for, right? — but instead of getting words on paper, or at least the computer screen, I thought about Daria Dattillo. She was such an odd person. So quiet. So self-effacing. Not at all like the image I had formed of her when first I met her. Was it really possible that she could turn out to be the new Emily Dickinson? I yanked open the bottom drawer of the desk where I had stashed the newspaper containing her poems, and I read them through again. Okay, so maybe they *were* good. Maybe they were even very good. Or did I just think so because I was being influenced by Ms. Peters? I ripped up the newspaper and spun around in my chair to toss it into the recycle bin beside my desk. As I swiveled, my elbow caught the can of pop and sent it cascading into the open drawer. Rats and double rats. The can had been almost full. Now the pop was spilling out all over the papers and notebooks in the drawer.

I grabbed the can first and tossed it into the garbage. Then I started picking out soggy papers: notes from stories I had already written or was planning to write, my science notebook — I didn't need a crystal ball to know there was recopying in my immediate future — a couple of *Reluctant Hero* magazines, all Coke-soaked to one degree or another. The only thing that had survived unscathed was the sheaf of notes left behind by the late Anna Maria Dattillo. I yanked them out, intending to finally throw them into the garbage to punish them for remaining pristine while things I cared about were stained and wrinkled. But something stopped me. A phrase. An astonishingly familiar phrase.

I got up and dug in the soggy papers in the recycle bin for the newspaper I had thrown there. After smoothing out and taping together the page containing Daria's poems, I read through one of them again. Interesting. Several of the phrases that appeared in Anna Maria Dattillo's notes reappeared in Daria's poems. I don't know exactly how the muse works, but I know enough about sisters to know that they don't think that much alike. And yet here in Daria's poetry was the echo of Anna Maria's poetry. Coincidence? Or had the great Daria Dattillo plagiarized her dead sister's work?

I suddenly felt better about my sonnet. At least it hadn't been stolen from anyone.

# Chapter 9

"I don't know what she wanted, Chloe," my mother said. She was standing at the sink, peeling carrots. Levesque was parked in front of the stove, shirt sleeves rolled up, chef's apron tied around his middle, stirring a pot of what looked like his famous spaghetti sauce. I'm not sure who had declared it famous or what exactly it was famous for, but it sure tasted good. "She called and asked me to ask you if you could stop by her house as soon as you had a few minutes. You have time to run over there before supper, if you want to."

*She* was Mrs. Flosnick, and, frankly, I didn't want to run over there. If I kept dashing off to Peter Flosnick's house, people were going to get the wrong idea about Peter and me.

"But, Mom," I said, feeling like a character caught in a tape loop — how many times had I said this, and to how many people? — "I hardly knew the guy. I spoke to him a grand total of maybe twice. I've spoken to his mother more than I ever talked to him."

My mother gave me one of her come-on-now-be-a-good-girl looks.

"Mrs. Flosnick is having a — "

" — hard time. I know, Mom. But — "

Levesque pulled his attention away from his

sauce to say, "No one's asking you to wade through a river full of crocodiles, Chloe." True enough, no one was. Thank you for clarifying the situation, but exactly how was this relevant? "Take ten minutes out of your busy life and find out what the woman wants, okay?"

He did that sometimes, he said "Okay?" like it was a question, like you had the option of saying, "No, thanks, I'd rather not." But it wasn't a question, and there was no option within a thousand miles.

"When's supper?" I asked.

"You have time," my mother said.

I was annoyed as I trudged over to Mrs. Flosnick's house. I was still annoyed as I climbed the steps to her front porch. My annoyance had not subsided one bit as I pressed her doorbell. At first I had been annoyed with Mrs. Flosnick. I had wanted to scream at her, read my lips: I did not know your son! But that feeling passed, and I was annoyed with myself instead. Levesque was right — it hurt whenever I had to admit that — the woman had just lost her only son. I could spare her a few minutes and a little compassion, couldn't I? And if I couldn't, what miserable thing did that say about me? I made sure I had a sympathetic smile on my face when I heard footsteps coming toward the door. It turned out it wasn't Mrs. Flosnick who was treated to my smile, though. Instead, Eileen Braden opened the door and peered out at me through the screen.

"Yes?"

"Is Mrs. Flosnick in?"

Eileen Braden leaned forward and squinted at me.

"You're Chloe, aren't you? Come in." She opened the screen door. "Elizabeth just ran to the store. She should be back in a minute."

"It's okay," I said. "I can drop by again later."

"Nonsense," Eileen Braden said, giving the word brisk, firm authority. Every teacher I've ever had or have ever met said that word the same way. It must be part of the curriculum at teachers' college. "You've already taken the trouble to come over here. Step inside. Really, she'll be right back."

Again I had no option. In I went, following her to the living room, which was dominated by one of those big-screen TV sets and three shelves of video-tapes. Most of their spines were hand-lettered. Someone in the house obviously did a lot of home taping.

"Elizabeth volunteers a couple of afternoons a week at the hospital, so she tapes her soap operas for watching in the evenings," Eileen Braden said.

I felt as if I had been caught snooping.

"Would you like a cup of tea?" she asked. A plain brown teapot stood in the middle of the coffee table. A mug of clear tea sat next to it.

"No, thanks."

"You don't mind if I finish mine, do you?"

"Oh, no."

"Please," she said. "Sit down."

I sat, then she sat across from me and sipped her tea.

"Elizabeth tells me that your family is new in town."

"We've been here for a couple of months."

"But you know who I am." It was a statement, not a question. A real Levesque maneuver. Since my face had probably already betrayed me, there seemed to be no reason to lie.

"I've heard your name," I told her.

She sighed. "Even when the mines were working flat out, this town was too small. Everyone knows everyone else and everyone makes it their business to know everyone else's business. I'm glad I moved to Morrisville."

"Morrisville isn't much bigger than East Hastings," I said.

"No, but it's far enough away that everyone didn't know every detail of my life when I got there. I was able to start all over, on my terms."

I figured she was referring to what had happened with Lise's father, but I wasn't about to ask.

She looked at me over the rim of her mug as she took another sip of tea.

"You must be in the same grade as Lise Arsenault."

Aha, I thought, as I nodded.

"How is she?"

"Lise? I don't know her very well, but I guess she's okay."

"And her father?"

What was that look in her eyes? It was soft and sort of sad. If I'd had to guess, I would have said Eileen Braden was still very much interested in Paul Arsenault.

"I've never met Mr. Arsenault," I said.

"Oh." She looked down into her mug. I couldn't tell what she was thinking. Then I heard the front door open and Eileen Braden jumped to her feet. "Elizabeth," she called, "you have company."

Mrs. Flosnick appeared in the kitchen with two plastic bags full of groceries, which she set down the moment she saw me.

"Chloe," she said, so warmly that if I didn't know better I would have thought I must be a close friend of the family. "I'm so glad you could come."

"No problem."

"And I see you've met my dear friend Eileen Braden. Eileen used to teach at East Hastings Regional High."

Neither Eileen nor I said anything.

"Well, I suppose I should get to the point," Mrs. Flosnick said. "I don't want to keep you from your dinner." Having said that, she abruptly left the room. I glanced over at Eileen Braden, who only shrugged in reply. A moment later Mrs. Flosnick was back, carrying one of the small cardboard boxes I had delivered to her only a few days ago.

"I found a lot of letters addressed to Peter at the school newspaper office among the things you brought me. I really think they should be returned to the newspaper."

I opened my mouth to say that the newspaper considered those letters Peter's private property, but, really, what was the point? If Mrs. Flosnick didn't want them and Ross didn't want them, I would just dump them. No one would know, no one would care and, best of all, I wouldn't have to argue or try to explain anything to anyone.

"I also put some of Peter's favorite books in there for you, Chloe."

Huh?

"He told me you're a great reader."

"I am," I said, but I was confused. How had Peter Flosnick known my reading habits? He must have been watching me when I wasn't looking.

"It's a shame to waste a good book, isn't that right, Eileen?" Mrs. Flosnick said. "I've kept most of Peter's books from when he was a little boy. I just can't bear to part with his copy of *Where the Wild Things Are* or *Winnie the Pooh*. But I'm sure he would have wanted you to have some of his favorites, too. He spoke about you so often."

What on earth had he told his mother about me? What could he possibly have said? He didn't know me any better than I knew him. Did he?

She handed the box to me. "Perhaps when you read one of Peter's books, you'll remember him and have a kind thought."

*If* I ever read one of weird Peter's books, I would *definitely* remember him. I wasn't sure what I would be thinking would be entirely kind, though.

"Oh, and could you tell that girl, oh dear, what

was her name? Mara? Dara?"

"Daria?" I said.

Mrs. Flosnick smiled. "That's it. Daria. Such a nice girl. She's a friend of yours, isn't she?"

Hey, why not? If I could count Peter Flosnick among my friends, I supposed I could include Daria, too. I nodded.

"Could you tell her for me that I couldn't find that notebook she was looking for. I went through all of Peter's things, but it wasn't there. If Peter borrowed some notes from her, he must have returned them."

"I'll tell her."

"I'm sorry I didn't get to meet Peter's friends under happier circumstances," Mrs. Flosnick said. "I had no idea he had so many of them. I always thought of him as something of a loner. It used to worry me, you know?" Here she glanced at Eileen Braden, who nodded. "He spoke of you often, of course. But I didn't even know about Daria. And then to find out that that nice Matthew Walker shares his interest in astronomy — "

"He does?" This was news to me.

"He most certainly does," Mrs. Flosnick said. "He was over here this afternoon. He wanted to borrow the videos Peter made of the stars at night. I gave him a whole box of the tapes Peter keeps — kept — in his room. I'm glad someone will enjoy them."

I was having trouble imagining Matt Walker gazing at the night sky, let alone gazing at videotape after videotape of it.

"I really have to be going, Mrs. Flosnick."

She smiled and saw me to the door. When I got home I took the box up to my room and shoved it into the back of my closet. Then I went downstairs and enjoyed two helpings of spaghetti with Levesque's famous sauce and two servings of Mom's not-so-famous but still good carrot salad.

\* \* \*

"We're all hooking up at Matt's," Thomas had told me. "Meet me over there and we'll head out together." We were heading over to Morrisville for a concert. Matt was driving. Driving, but not picking up.

There are some things you don't really find out about people until you get to know them. Their tendency to be late or on time is a good example. I arrived on Matt's doorstep ten minutes late, on purpose. I didn't know him very well yet, so I wanted to be the last person to arrive, not the first. That's when I found out that, in this crowd, ten minutes late meant crossing the finish line first.

Mrs. Walker — er, Lambton — answered the door. "Matt's down in the basement," she said as she stood aside to let me in. "Go on down."

I hesitated. I sure didn't know Matt well enough to barge in on him. But Mrs. Lambton was standing behind me, watching me expectantly, smiling at me, so I started down the stairs.

"Hello?" I called after I'd taken the first few steps.

"Hey, hi!" came a voice. Matt's voice. "Tommy, that you?"

I don't think that he mistook my voice for Thomas's, but I'll bet that he thought if I was there, Thomas must be with me.

"It's Chloe," I said.

He was sprawled on a sofa when I reached the bottom step. Or, more accurately, he had been sprawled on the couch — all the cushions were out of place — and now he was scrambling for something. I glanced at the TV. What naughty thing had he been watching that he didn't want anyone to see? Anyone female, that is. Imagine my surprise when all I saw was a blank screen. No, make that a dark screen. Like . . . a night sky.

"That's one of Peter's tapes, isn't it?" I asked.

He stared at me as if I had just divined his middle name.

"Yeah," he said. I think the word just popped out, because as soon as he had said it, he looked pained, as if he wished he had said something different. "Yeah, it is."

"Is it interesting?"

He finally found the remote and used it to shut off the TV.

"No," he said. "It's one big yawn."

Really? Let's push a button and see what happens. "Mrs. Flosnick told me that you share Peter's passion for astronomy. That was sure news to me."

Now he stared at me as if I had just divined his middle name and it had turned out to be Beverley or Evelyn.

"Mrs. Flosnick told you that?"

106

"She said that's what you told her."

"Yeah, well, the guy was weird." He tossed the remote onto the table and glanced at his watch. "Where is everyone? We're going to be late."

"Why did you lie to Mrs. Flosnick?" I asked.

"Who says I lied?"

"Name the brightest star in Ursa Major."

He looked confused.

"You're a real astronomy buff all right," I said. "Why did you lie to Mrs. Flosnick?"

He stiffened up. "What's it to you?"

"She's a nice lady." She really was. It wasn't her fault her son was a geek. "She thinks you were Peter's friend. It made her happy to think that. Now I'm going to have to tell her it isn't true."

"You don't have to tell her anything," Matt said. "You could just keep your nose out of other people's business."

I just stared at him. It was a little trick I had learned from Levesque. Keep quiet, keep still, keep watch . . . and see what happens.

"Okay, so I was curious," Matt finally said. "What's that, some kind of a crime? The guy was always staring out his window with that expensive telescope of his. I just wanted to see what he was staring at, that's all. I'm going to give back the tapes. It isn't like I stole them or anything. I asked her if I could borrow them and she said sure."

"Hey, Matt!" someone called from the top of the stairs. It sounded like Thomas. "Come on, we're late."

Matt zoomed by me so fast he almost bowled me over. I followed him more slowly up the stairs. Thomas, Lise and Daria were waiting at the top. Thomas smiled when he saw me and slipped his arm around my waist. I forgot all about Matt and Mrs. Flosnick and was happy to settle into the back seat of Matt's car beside Thomas. I didn't even care that Daria shared the back seat with us.

It took a little less than an hour to get to Morrisville, but it seemed like a lot longer because Lise kept fretting that we were going to be late, that we were going to get bad seats, but even then she kept nagging at Matt not to speed. It was a bit of a surprise, then, that when we finally got to Morrisville and were only a few blocks away from the arena, Lise suddenly shouted, "Stop the car!"

# Chapter 10

Matt didn't react at first. Maybe he thought Lise was kidding. I know I did. But she quickly blitzed that notion by screaming again for Matt to stop the car, and this time he did what he was told.

"What the — " he started, but broke off when Lise shoved open the car door and jumped out. She didn't go anywhere, though. She just stood beside the car. I didn't get it. Then Daria said, "Oh," and something in the way she said it told me that she had figured out what was going on.

"What?" Thomas said. He leaned across me to look where Daria was pointing. I looked too, but all I saw was a small-town main street and a bunch of small town people coming out of shops or going into them or just strolling around. Then something strange happened. When you're in a place you've never visited before, the last thing you expect is to see someone you know. But that's what happened. I saw someone I knew. Well, sort of knew. There, across the street, was Eileen Braden. She was talking to a man. A friend, I assumed, or a neighbor . . . I turned out to be wrong.

"That's Paul Arsenault," Thomas told me. "Lise's father."

*Très intéressant,* as we used to say back home.

Lise jumped back into the car as abruptly as she

had left it and scrunched down in the front seat. She was hiding, I realized.

"Let's get out of here," she hissed at Matt.

Matt, ever the perfect boyfriend, nodded. "Whatever you say."

Lise didn't say a word the rest of the way to the arena. No one else spoke, either. Well, no one except Matt, and all he said were things like, "Here we are," and, "Think we'll find parking?" and, "Guess we'd better get inside if we're going to get a seat." Fill-the-awkward-gaps talk.

We did find a parking space, and a few minutes later we were making our way through the shallow entrance area and into the crowded interior of the arena. We finally found some not-so-great seats near the back. Who had dreamed up the idea of general admission seating for concerts? I wished I had brought a pair of binoculars so that I could at least see the stage. Then I remembered that I had never heard of the band that was playing — it was home-grown — so it didn't really matter.

No sooner had we sat down than Lise popped up again and announced she was going to the bathroom. Daria ran after her as if she were attached to Lise by an invisible wire. Matt gave me a sour look and said, "I'm going to get a soda. You want one, Thomas?" Notice he didn't ask me. I guess he was still mad at me for quizzing him about the tapes.

"Finally," said Thomas, leaning back in his seat and sliding an arm around my shoulder. "This is going to be great."

Was he kidding? Hadn't he noticed what was going on? I peered at him and he started to laugh.

"Okay, so some people aren't happy and well-adjusted," he said. "But other people are so happy and so well-adjusted they should be winning mental health prizes."

"People like you, I suppose?"

"And like you."

"And by well-adjusted you mean . . . ?"

"We don't let other people's problems ruin our fun."

I ran that one through the brain circuits for a minute. "That's an interesting definition of the word. You realize, I suppose, that some people might find that a little — hmm, how can I put this nicely? — a little selfish."

"Selfish?" The idea seemed to astonish him.

"As in self-centered. Self-absorbed."

He waved his hand dismissively. "I prefer to think of it as focused."

I couldn't help it. I laughed. "Focused on yourself, you mean."

Matt returned just in time for the start of the concert. Lise and Daria didn't. Matt twisted this way and that, obviously looking for Lise. Then he leaned over and whispered something in Thomas's ear. Thomas, in turn, leaned over to me and said, "I don't suppose you'd like to check out the ladies' room and see what Lise and Daria are up to." I didn't suppose I would. "Matt's worried," Thomas added, when I didn't move. Matt was sitting right next to Thomas. He could easily have explained this to me himself. Some people would have said that he *should* have explained it himself. "Lise has a tendency to get worked up where her father and Eileen Braden are concerned," Thomas explained. "Please? As a special favor to me?"

I know for a fact that I wouldn't have gone out hunting the Empty-Headed Queens even if Matt had gone down on his knees and begged me to. But for Thomas? Well, for Thomas I would have done just about anything.

"Do me a favor," I said as I squeezed by him. "Don't tell me what I missed."

Lise and Daria weren't in the ladies' room. They weren't at the snack bar. They weren't out in the area near the front doors. Which only left outside the arena. I pushed open the door and stood for a moment in the cool night air. The parking lot was dark except for the evenly spaced circular pools of brightness cast by the lights on top of a dozen or so stands. At first glance, it seemed pretty much empty. I didn't look for the Queens as much as listen for them. After a moment I heard Lise's voice.

"They all think she's so nice, but she isn't. She's a conniving, manipulative, greedy — "

Oh great, I thought. Lise had come outside to rag on me. Then I heard Daria say, "Your father obviously doesn't feel that way."

Okay, big relief. They weren't talking about me after all.

I zeroed in on their voices and finally located

them next to a lamppost near where Matt had parked his car. I crept a little closer, but didn't declare my presence.

"But he dumped her," Lise said. "*He* dumped *her*. So what is he doing here with her now? And why didn't he tell me he was going to see her?"

By now I understood that she was talking about her father and Eileen Braden.

"Maybe because he knows you don't like her," Daria said.

"But she cheated on him when they were going together. He had proof of it and it really hurt him. He took it almost as hard as when Mom left." Lise sounded bitter as she said this. "When he saw for a fact that she had been cheating on him, he dumped her. Why would he take up with her again? Especially when Mom is planning to come for a visit?"

"I thought he didn't know your mother was coming," Daria said.

"What does that have to do with anything? He shouldn't be seeing Eileen Braden. She broke his heart."

"Who says he's actually seeing her?" Daria said. "Besides, didn't you say you heard that she was engaged?"

"Yeah . . . " Lise said, but her voice trembled and — I might have been wrong — but I didn't think it was just because of the cold. "And I told my father that I heard it. He was depressed for a week."

Nice daughter, I thought, telling her father something she must have known would upset him.

"But?" Daria said. She must have picked up on Lise's tone too.

"How was I supposed to know it was just a rumor?" Lise said angrily.

"A rumor started by you?"

Lise didn't answer the question. Instead she said, "He never comes to Morrisville. What's he doing here now?"

I heard a little sigh. "By now he probably knows she isn't engaged," Daria said.

"He can't possibly be planning to get back together with her," Lise moaned. "Can he?"

"I guess it's possible that he still loves her," Daria said.

For a moment neither of them said anything. Then Lise spoke. "I don't get it. She's not anything like my mom."

"Maybe you should just leave them alone, you know? Lise?" Daria said. She said it nicely, like a real friend who was trying to pass along some good advice. But it was apparently the wrong thing to say, because Lise's voice grew shrill.

"Maybe you should butt out! He *dumped* her. That was the whole point."

"The whole point of what?"

But Lise didn't answer. Instead she said, "If he dumped her once, he can dump her again."

"Lise, I don't really think — "

"If you're going to be negative, I'm not listening," Lise said.

Very nice. If that was the way she treated her best friend, I suppose I shouldn't feel bad about the way she treated me. She wheeled away from Daria. As she did, she spied me. Her already angry expression soured into a scowl as she marched past me into the arena. Daria glanced at me, but just shrugged. She scurried after Lise without bothering to see if I was following. Someone could have been mugging me right there in a pool of light for all anyone cared. I decided then and there that that was the last time I would ever do a favor for Matt Walker.

* * *

It's hard to have a great time when almost everyone around you is in a bad mood. Lise was angry because she had seen her father with Eileen Braden. Matt was annoyed because Lise was in a bad mood and wouldn't let him put his arm around her. Daria was upset because Lise was upset — I guess it must have had something to do with her sympathetic poet's soul. And I was ticked off because I was sick of Lise looking down her nose at me and tired of Daria steering a wide course around me as if she were some great sailing ship and I was a reef that was just waiting to wreck her. Thomas was the only one who seemed to be having a good time. He bounced and shook to the music, and sang along with most of the numbers. What he lacked in vocal ability he more than made up for in enthusiasm.

When the concert was finally over, Matt and

Thomas wanted to get something to eat. Lise was still sulking. She grabbed a window booth at the restaurant, and while I made the happy discovery that the Morrisville version of Stella's Great Home Cooking not only had heard of cappuccino, but was able to produce a cup for me, Lise was peering out the window, looking, no doubt, for her father. She didn't take her eyes off the street the whole time we were there. Daria didn't take her eyes off Lise.

In the awkward silence, I suddenly remembered my promise to Peter's mother. "Daria, Mrs. Flosnick asked me to tell you that she looked everywhere, but she couldn't find your notebook in Peter's things. She said Peter must have returned it to you."

Daria said nothing. She barely even looked at me.

"What notebook is that, Dare?" Matt asked. "And how come you loaned a notebook to that loser?"

"It was my history notebook," Daria said. She squirmed in her seat. "He missed a class a couple of weeks ago and he asked me if he could copy my notes."

"And you said yes?" Matt seemed to be having trouble understanding this.

Daria shrugged. "He pestered me."

"Why would he pester you?" I asked. Peter must have known what Daria thought of him. Wouldn't he have asked someone a little less contemptuous of him?

"I don't know," Daria said. She sounded annoyed.

"He just did. And I figured it was easier to say yes than to have him following me around asking me over and over again. Then after I loaned it to him, he kept it forever. So I went and asked his mother for it."

"She couldn't find it," I said.

Suddenly Daria's eyes were sharp on me. Bye-bye shy, retiring poet.

"So you said."

Lise jumped up and struggled to push by Matt.

"Hey," he protested, "what's the rush? Where you going?" Then, "Oh." He grabbed her arm and tried to hold her. "What are you planning to do, Lise? Make a big scene in the middle of the street? You think that's what your dad wants?"

I glanced out the window. Eileen Braden and Paul Arsenault were standing on the sidewalk on the other side of the street. They weren't exactly holding hands, but their hands were touching. You know, brushing against each other. Whatever differences they may have had in the past, they seemed to have moved on.

"Let me by, Matt," Lise said. She looked like she was ready to smack him if he refused.

"No way. Your dad's not going to like it if you butt into his relationship."

"That's really funny, coming from you," Lise said. "You always interfered in your mother's relationship with Artie and you didn't care what your mother thought about it. And you haven't let up yet, have you?"

"That's different," Matt said. "Artie's a creep. Miss Braden's okay."

"Let me by."

"It would be a big mistake, Lise."

She was suddenly very still. She looked down at Matt with the coldest eyes I have ever seen.

"Who asked you?" she said.

Matt threw up his arms. "Fine, go ahead. Make a fool of yourself. Make your father furious. Go right ahead!"

He slid out of the booth and stood well back to let her pass. When he sat down again, he pounded the table so hard with his fist that the glass vinegar bottle and the plastic ketchup container actually cleared the table. The rest of us looked out the window.

Lise raced across the street. She was calling her father as she went. He looked up and saw her coming. Stiffened. His hand left the vicinity of Eileen Braden's hand. He stepped back a pace. It was exactly the kind of thing Lise might have done if her father had appeared unexpectedly on a street corner where she and Matt were talking and holding hands. Except that Lise's father didn't look sheepish about being caught, nor did he seem to be offering any apologies for his actions. Then, as quickly as he had backed away from Eileen Braden, he was beside her again, sheltering her in his arm, shepherding her away from Lise. Then he said something to Lise, his face scowling. It wasn't hard to imagine that it was something like, "I'll see you at home, young lady."

Lise was left standing alone on the sidewalk. She pounded her fist into a mailbox. As if summoned, Matt slid out of the booth and raced across the street to join her. Daria followed. Thomas sighed and dug in his pocket for his wallet. He threw some money on the table and turned to me.

"Shall we?"

I wished we didn't have to, but, "Sure."

By the time Thomas and I got there, Matt had his arm around Lise and was trying to calm her. Lise, of course, was refusing to be calmed. She kept saying, "He wasn't supposed to see her again. She was supposed to go away and that was supposed to be that."

Maybe. But *suppose* obviously had nothing to do with it.

By the time Matt pulled his car up in front of my house, I had had it with the whole bunch of them. Well, maybe not Thomas. But the rest of them.

Thomas got out of the car and walked me up to the house. The living room light was on inside. Levesque or my mom, maybe even both of them, were waiting up for me.

"I hope you had a good time," Thomas said.

"I did." I would have had a much better time without his friends, but I didn't tell him that. "Thanks for inviting me."

"Thanks for coming."

We stood on the steps for a moment, peering into each other's eyes. I knew that my mother was

119

inside. I knew that his friends were in the car watching us. It was a classic end-of-date, awkward moment. Then he leaned forward and kissed me on the lips. He didn't rush it, and he didn't overplay it either. It was sweet and warm and delicious. Then it was over.

Levesque was sitting in the living room, reading the newspaper, when I came in.

"Did you have a good time?" he asked.

I nodded. "'Night."

"Sleep well."

But I couldn't sleep at all. Everything kept bumping around in my brain — Lise and her obsession with her father's love life (grow up, Lise), Daria lending a notebook to Peter Flosnick, Matt and his obvious dislike of me, Thomas and his smile and his lips and the way he sang along with the music, the way he didn't care if he was on key or not, he just went with the moment. He knew how to enjoy himself.

After I had stared at the darkened ceiling in my room for fifteen or twenty minutes, I surrendered, turned on my light, and looked around for something to read, preferably something that I hadn't already read. That was when I started missing the Montreal Public Library system and wishing that the price of books didn't seem so outrageous in relation to my meager allowance. Then I remembered the stack of books that Mrs. Flosnick had given to me. I got up and pulled the box out of my closet.

It was an interesting collection: a novel by Carl Sagan, which I set aside (I wasn't sure sci-fi was for me); two novels by William Faulkner (I love Faulkner. Had Peter really read these books? They looked well-thumbed enough. I almost began to regret that I had never had a conversation with Peter); a copy of *The Catcher in the Rye* (I had already read it — three times); a couple of more modern novels by writers I had never heard of, but who, considering the Faulkners and the Salinger, I decided I should check out. Then there was the Poe. I had read a few short stories by old Edgar Allan — who hadn't? They were okay. Not the kind of thing I'd rave over, but passable. So why did I pick that book out of the box and carry it back to my bed? I don't know. But I did. I read a few stories. And they did the trick.

# Chapter 11

I hadn't been thrilled when Mom announced that she was going to marry Levesque. Problem number one — my mother didn't exactly have the best track record with men. She had been married twice already, and neither of those relationships had lasted more than a few years. It was hard to believe that after digging up buckets of fool's gold that she had finally hit the mother lode. Problem number two — the guy was a cop. Now really, who would want to spend years of their life being scrutinized by someone who wormed the truth out of people for a living? What kind of fun would that be? Problem number three — Phoebe adored Levesque. She liked him right from the start and started calling him Dad before it was even legal. You just know that if Phoebe likes something, there has to be something wrong with it.

So, sure, I admit it, I didn't *want* Mom to marry Levesque. But I didn't try to stop her, either. The way I looked at it, Mom falling for Levesque wasn't much different from her deciding to paint the entire house fluorescent pink. It affected me in that I had to live with it and look at it every day. But the effect was purely external and it promised to be relatively short-term: It wasn't as if I was going to live in that house forever. And, like even the worst decorating *faux pas*, Levesque kind of grew on you. He may not have been my first choice to star in the role of my stepdad, but he turned out to be better than adequate in the part. Sometimes you have to give things a chance.

All of which is to say that I thought Lise was overreacting. She showed up at school on Monday ecstatic. Her eyes shone, she had a big grin on her face, and she couldn't stop talking. She and Matt must have made up, I thought at first. I was wrong.

"My dad and I drove down to Toronto on Saturday," she said. "We spent the whole weekend together. We went shopping along Queen Street and he took me to this great restaurant for dinner. Then we went to a play. It was just the two of us and it was great!"

Great.

By noon, though, when she found us in the cafeteria, she had crashed. No more grin, no more wide, happy eyes, just a lot of frantic talk.

"He's not in his office. I called three times, and he's not there," she said. Not to me, of course, but to Daria and Matt and Thomas.

"Who's not there?" Matt asked.

"My father, stupid." Ah, the sweet sound of people in love.

"He probably went for lunch."

"His secretary says he's out for the rest of the day."

"Maybe he had to go to a meeting," Daria suggested.

"If he had to go to a meeting, he would have told his secretary. But she told me he didn't say where he was going."

"Big deal," Thomas said. "Maybe he's playing hooky for the afternoon. Way to go, Paul!"

Lise looked as if she wanted to slap him.

"What if he drove up to Morrisville?" she said. "What if he went to see *her* again?"

Matt rolled his eyes as if to say, not *that* again. "In her classroom?"

"Maybe she took the day off."

"What if she did? Come on, Lise, lighten up. Let the guy have a little happiness."

Now she looked as if she wanted to smack Matt.

"You don't understand," she said. Actually, she shouted it. "You don't understand anything!"

Matt stiffened. "I'm getting a little tired of hearing that," he said.

"Then I suggest you keep your stupid opinions to yourself."

Matt glowered at her. "I can do better than that," he said. He stood up abruptly, almost toppling the pile of textbooks and notebooks Daria had stacked on the table. She had to scramble to keep them from falling over. "If you don't want to listen to what I have to say, fine!" He glanced at Thomas. "Come on, let's get out of here."

Thomas looked at me and shrugged. I knew that look: *He's my friend and I have to see what I can do to calm him down, okay?* I nodded. Thomas loped out of the cafeteria at Matt's heels.

"Idiot," Lise muttered.

"He was just trying to put things in perspective," Daria said quietly. "I mean, how would you like it if your dad tried to break up you and Matt?"

"This isn't the same thing at all," Lise said.

"What's different about it?"

The way Lise looked at Daria, you would have thought Daria had just grown a second head — a traitorous second head.

"What's the matter with everyone all of a sudden?" Lise said, standing up abruptly. "Don't any of you care about me? Don't you care about how I feel?" She slung her purse over her shoulder and started for the door.

Daria jumped up. "Lise, I — "

Lise spun around, her face tightened in rage. "Don't follow me," she hissed at Daria. It was one of those really loud hisses, the kind that's guaranteed to attract the attention of everyone in the room, even if it's a large room like a cafeteria. "Don't you *dare* follow me."

Daria slumped back down into her seat. She kept her head down. Maybe she was trying to ignore the people who were still staring in our direction, trying to figure out what had just happened. She silently gathered the remains of everyone's lunches onto her tray. She looked at me only once, and when she did, I saw tears glistening in her eyes. Maybe they blurred her vision, I don't know, but when she finally stood up and reached for her stack of books, she knocked them over. She let out a whimper of frustration as they cascaded to the floor. One of her notebooks slipped under the table, close to me, and I leaned over to scoop it up. By the time I straightened up again, Daria had retrieved the rest of her books, gathered them into her arms and was hurrying out of the cafeteria. I started to get up to dash after her, then I thought, why should I go out of my way to help her? I'd give her back her notebook the next time I saw her.

I don't know what made me look inside the notebook. Maybe it was the word HISTORY printed neatly on the cover. I opened it and looked at the first page. The date had been entered on the first line. In fact, I noticed as I went through page after page, Daria always wrote the date before she started taking notes. Monday, September 11. Tuesday, September 12. Wednesday, September 13. Day after day, without fail. Interesting.

I found her at her locker after school. "This isn't the history notebook you were asking Mrs. Flosnick for, is it?" I asked her.

Bye-bye sad, sensitive face. Hello glare. The gentle poet looked suddenly fierce. She reached out to grab the notebook from me. I jerked it back out of her reach.

"It's so nice and neat," I said. "And so organized, too. I notice that you write in the date every day."

"Give me that!"

"And, lookee here," I said, flipping through the pages, "there isn't a single date missing since the beginning of school."

There's a story you hear all the time. I don't know if it's true or not, but it goes something like this: An ordinary man is traveling in his car with his son from Point A to Point B. When he's halfway there, he's involved in an accident. His car flips over. He manages to escape the vehicle unhurt. But his child is trapped inside the car and the car's engine is on fire. In a few seconds the fire will spread to the fuel line and the car will explode. This ordinary man — maybe he's even your classic ninety-eight-pound weakling — by sheer will and necessity, suddenly takes on the strength of an entire army. He manages, single-handedly, to upright the car and pull his child free just moments before the whole car goes off like a bomb.

Daria is a small, pale, slight thing. She may or may not have been plagiarizing her sister's poems, but she was everyone's physical stereotype of an *artiste*. She even looked poetic. But she leapt at me like a December 26th bargain hunter bent on snagging that last ninety-percent-off pair of Gap khakis, and wrenched the book from my hand with such force that I pulled a muscle just trying to keep from collapsing under her weight. She shoved the book onto the top shelf of her locker, slammed the door, locked it, then wheeled around and marched away, which left me standing in the hallway thinking what I had been thinking in the cafeteria earlier in the day — that there was no way that notebook had been out of Daria's possession for a day, let alone the week or more she claimed it had been in Peter's possession. Not one date had been missing. So when she had gone over to Peter Flosnick's house to ask Peter's mother for her notebook back, what had she *really* been looking for?

* * *

Thomas was sorry, he said, but he couldn't see me after school. "Matt needs some chill time," he explained. "You understand."

Matt needed some chill time? I needed some chill time. More. I needed to go back to Montreal. I needed my old friends, who were normal and who focused on their own lives, who frankly couldn't care less what their parents were up to so long as it didn't interfere with their weekends. But Montreal might as well have been on the other side of the Pacific Ocean for all the good it did me. No e-mail at our house. Mom was a dragon lady when it came to running up a phone bill. Besides, whining to someone hundreds of miles away wasn't going to change the fact that I lived here now, surrounded by a whole new townful of people. So, since I couldn't go there, I went to my room instead. Went inside, closed the door, turned on some music really loud and flopped down onto my bed. Thomas was great. I loved Thomas. Well, not really loved him, not romantically. Not yet, anyway. But he was fun to be around, and compared to the rest of the head cases up here, he was okay. Level-headed. Pleasant. Charming, even. His friends were another story. I wondered what my chances were of weaning him away from that crowd.

After a while I scooped up the book on my bedside table — Peter's Edgar Allan Poe book — and started to read. If it had been a couple of years ago, you couldn't have forced that book on me at gunpoint. A couple of years ago, I wasn't much of a reader. Then one day, for lack of something better to do, I picked up a book and started reading and I haven't stopped since. Relatively recent stuff at first. Then I started moving backward in time — *Lives of Girls and Women*, *The Catcher in the Rye*, *To Kill a Mockingbird*. Then I started getting curious about all those books you always hear about but don't actually know anyone who's read them — books like *The Grapes of Wrath*, *East of Eden*, *A Farewell to Arms* — and I started reading those, too. For a long time I avoided the really old books, you know, the ones written in that stuffy-sounding English from a hundred or so years ago. Books like, well, like Poe. Books with sentences like, "I was sick — sick unto death with that long agony . . . " Now, sometimes, I read those too.

Poe is okay. Not great, but interesting — in my opinion. Peter, I guess, had a different opinion. His copy of the book was dog-eared and lots of passages had been underlined. As I got deeper into it I started to notice scribbles in the margins. In one story in particular, "The Purloined Letter," — I had to look up the word "purloined" — the inside margins were filled with jottings, numbers mostly, although there was a series of letters at the top of each little column of numbers. For example, on one page, penciled into the margin near the top of page, was AMW. Then, underneath: 100-04-01, 50-10-02, 50-30-02 and on and on. There were maybe twenty sets of numbers on the page altogether. On another page were the letters BDD, followed by another set of numbers. It was like a little puzzle, and I spent a few minutes trying to figure it out. I scanned the page to see where the letters AMW appeared. They didn't, not together like that. I counted the letters on the page — the hundredth, the fourth, the first, and got the word "gtj." Then I remembered that Peter was a star nut. Maybe he had used this book, which, judging from the wear and tear on the binding, was one of his favorites, to make some kind of star notes. I forgot his scribblings and concentrated on the story again, and the more I read, the less I thought about Lise and Daria and Matt, and the better I felt.

* * *

Thomas was distracted.

When you're out with a guy, especially when he takes you down to the shore of a crystal clear lake on a beautiful, starry night, you want to be the focal point of the guy's attention. You don't want him thinking about ten other things. Actually, you don't even want him thinking about one other thing.

"Worrying about Matt?" I asked. When I had last seen him, he had been scurrying after Matt to comfort him.

"Worrying about Lise," he replied. "Matt's worried about her, too, but he's not nearly as worried as me."

Terrific. When you're out with a guy, you don't want to know that he's thinking about another girl, especially if the girl in question is his ex-girlfriend. You certainly don't want to hear that he's more concerned about this ex-girlfriend than her current boyfriend is.

"She's acting crazy again," he said.

"Again?" Surely he meant, still, I thought, but I didn't say it. It would have sounded too catty.

He sat down on a big rock and gazed out over the lake. I stood facing him, waiting for an explanation and thinking, this had better be good.

"I'm afraid she's going to do something stupid," he said. "Lise and I — " He paused and looked up at me a little nervously. "I used to go out with her."

"Yeah, I know."

"Oh." He peered at me, looking for — what? Approval? Disapproval? I tried not to show anything. If he was going to spend *our* evening talking about his ex-girlfriend, he deserved to keep guessing. "I was going out with her when her dad started seeing Eileen."

Yeah, and? I didn't say anything, but my face must have given away the fact that not only did I not want to talk about Lise Arsenault, I didn't even care about her.

"You don't understand," he said.

"Enlighten me."

He sighed. "I'm making a mess of all this, aren't

I?" He sounded so miserable that my sense of pity finally kicked in.

"Okay," I said. "Tell me what's bothering you."

"You don't mind?"

"I don't mind as long as you promise we're not going to talk about Lise every time we go out."

He smiled. "I promise." Then, after a deep breath, "Lise's father didn't start seeing Eileen Braden until almost two years after his divorce from Lise's mother. It didn't seem like such a big deal to me. You can't expect a guy to be a monk for the rest of his life, right?"

"Right." If he said so.

"And Eileen is okay. She's nice, you know? And it wasn't her fault that Lise's mother took off. But Lise didn't see it that way. I couldn't believe how obsessed she was with trying to break them up. It was like I got a whole other look at her, at what kind of person she was. She used to say mean things about Eileen all the time. She used to make a big deal out of the fact that Eileen played bridge competitively and that her partner was a guy, a teacher from Morrisville."

"Was she involved with him, too?"

Thomas shook his head. "No. They were just friends. They played bridge together and as far as I know, that was the extent of their relationship. But Lise always made it seem like something else had to be going on. You know, why would a man and woman spend so much time together unless they were involved with each other?"

"Her father obviously agreed with her," I said. "Didn't you tell me he got jealous of her bridge partner and that's why they finally broke up?"

Thomas said nothing for a while. He just stared out over the water.

"Thomas, that *is* what you told me. Are you saying that's not what happened?"

"I'm not saying anything," he said.

Well, true enough. He was being downright uncommunicative on the point. "But that's what you think, isn't it?"

He turned back to me. "If I tell you something, do you promise you won't breathe a word to anyone?"

What could possibly be making him so serious?

"I promise," I said.

"Matt and Daria think the only reason Lise is acting so crazy now is because she's afraid Eileen Braden will mess up the chances of her dad getting back together with her mom when she comes to visit at Christmas."

"Well, isn't she?"

Thomas shook his head. "There's another reason."

I waited.

"Lise is terrified that if her father spends enough time with Eileen Braden, he'll also find out what Lise did."

"Which is what, exactly?"

A very long pause followed.

"Thomas?"

"She broke them up."

"Oh." Was that all? "Kids cause problems for divorced parents all the time. In fact, I read somewhere that stepchildren are the leading cause of second marriages breaking up. There have been whole books written on the subject."

"No, you don't get it," Thomas said. "I don't mean they broke up because Lise was acting like some kind of snotty little kid. I mean, she plotted to break them up, and she succeeded."

"Thomas, what are you talking about?"

"She tricked her father. She made him think something was true when it wasn't. And the worst part is, I think I helped her."

"What?"

"I made a tape for her."

"What kind of tape?"

There was a long pause before he answered.

"An audiotape. I thought it was some kind of joke. She brought her tape recorder over one day and she had written out all these things she wanted me to say, things a guy might say on the phone to a woman he was involved with. She got me to say them into the tape recorder in a deep voice. I didn't even recognize myself when she played it back."

"What did Lise do with the tape?"

"I don't know for sure." His eyes slipped away from mine and he looked out over the lake again. I circled around the rock he was sitting on so that I was between him and the water.

"If you don't want to tell me about this, fine," I

said. "But if you're going to tell me something, then tell me. Trust me. Don't act like I'm all of a sudden giving you the third degree, because I'm not. I didn't ask. You offered."

"Sorry," he said, looking straight at me now. "And you're right. I haven't told anyone about this, not even Matt. I'm not even sure why I'm telling you, except — "

"That you're worried about her and she's your ex-girlfriend, after all."

He looked startled. "No," he said, "that's not it at all. I mean, yeah, I'm worried about her. But I'm telling *you* because, well, because I like talking to you. Because I trust you."

I was flattered. Who wouldn't be when a guy you really like tells you things he hasn't even told his best friend?

"I'm pretty sure she used that tape that time her father and Eileen Braden went away for the weekend. I think she called the inn where they were staying and left messages for Eileen. I'm also pretty sure she called Eileen's house when her father was there and hung up if her father answered the phone, to make her father suspicious."

No one could have accused me of thinking very highly of Lise to begin with, but, "That's a pretty nasty thing to do to your own father," I said.

"Well . . . not if you think you're saving him from making a big mistake."

"But still — "

"I overheard her talking to another teacher at

school."

"Who? Lise?"

"No. Eileen Braden. I got sent up to the teachers' lounge one day to deliver a note to a teacher who was up there on a break, and when I got there the door was partway open and I heard Eileen Braden telling another teacher about the phone ringing when Paul was at her house but that whoever it was hung up when Paul answered. And the time she had come home with him once and had checked the messages on her machine and there was one from a man whose voice she didn't recognize, and she was embarrassed by the message and she told Paul it must be some kind of joke, but that she had the impression he didn't believe her. She said that he kept pressuring her to quit playing bridge but she refused — there was a big tournament coming up and she couldn't leave her partner in the lurch. Besides, she thought Paul was being arrogant to even ask her to quit. But the more she refused, the angrier he got. She was almost in tears, Chloe. She was telling this other teacher what had happened and she was choking back tears."

Thomas paused and looked up at me. "Then, about a week later, Lise told me that her father had broken up with Eileen. Apparently he had been at her house and flowers arrived with some kind of mushy, romantic note. The way Lise told it, Eileen tried to pretend that she thought the flowers were from her father. But they weren't. Paul was convinced they came from Eileen's bridge partner, which meant that Eileen was cheating on him. They had a big fight and broke up."

I digested this for a few moments. I suspected I was going to hate myself for what I was about to say, but how could I *not* say it? "You could have told Lise's father what you suspected," I told Thomas. "You could have saved him a lot of heartbreak."

He hung his head. "You think I haven't thought about that? But I didn't. And now either Lise is going to try to ruin things for them again, or she's going to make herself crazy worrying about being found out."

I shrugged. "That's what they call facing the music, Thomas. Or, you made your bed and now you have to lie in it. She did something stupid and now she has to pay for it. That's life." That probably sounded callous. But it was true.

"Yeah," Thomas said. He didn't sound as if he believed it. A little while later he walked me home. He kissed me, too, but his heart wasn't in it. Neither, frankly, was mine. He had helped Lise do something despicable. Maybe he hadn't known at the time what was going on. But when he had figured it out, he hadn't tried to do anything to make the situation right. Did I want a boyfriend who obviously didn't know right from wrong, or wouldn't act on it when he did know?

# Chapter 12

The next morning as I was leaving the house for school, Mom asked me to take the two bundles of old newspapers from the porch and put them down by the road for the recycling truck. No problem. I scooped up the top bundle, which was neatly tied with string, and started down the walk. That's when I noticed the headline: *Local Death: Suicide or Foul Play?* Underneath the words was a photo of Peter Flosnick. Hey, what was going on? I broke the string off the bundle, grabbed the top newspaper and read the brief article. As I read, I wondered why someone — especially a certain someone in my own family — hadn't said anything about this to me. That's when Levesque came down the walk behind me.

"I went to a lot of trouble to tie up those papers," he said. "If you wanted to read something in that bundle, you could at least have untied the string instead of breaking it. Now I'll have to go and get another piece."

I looked up from the article. "It says here that you're taking a second look at Peter Flosnick's death. It says you think it may not have been suicide after all."

Levesque looked faintly amused. "Does it?" he said. "That's interesting, because I was interviewed for that article and I could have sworn I said only that we were attempting to reconstruct the last hours of Peter Flosnick's life. I have no idea what led the reporter who interviewed me to decide that we had rejected the suicide theory."

"Theory?"

Levesque said nothing. Strike one.

"Why would you reconstruct Peter's last hours if you were sure it was suicide?" I asked.

He shrugged. "Elizabeth Flosnick doesn't believe her son killed himself. She's been contacting everyone she knows in the area — mayors, councilors, provincial and federal politicians. She's lived here for most of her life. She seems to know everyone there is to know."

"She putting pressure on you, you mean?" From what I had heard and read in the newspapers back home, this wouldn't be the first time that someone tried to pressure Levesque or influence one of his investigations. What *would* be a first was if Elizabeth Flosnick was having some success with her campaign.

"It never hurts to nose around a little," Levesque said. "Maybe we can find out more about what happened that day."

"What drove Peter to suicide, you mean?"

"Did I say that?"

It seemed to me that he was making a big effort not to say much of anything. He was talking, but he wasn't explaining. But that didn't mean that there wasn't something going on. Levesque had been investigating a murder when Mom met him. He had been on a few more homicide cases before we moved up here. I knew that look in his eyes, and I knew what it meant when he avoided saying things.

"There's something else that's making you look into this," I said. "Something besides Mrs. Flosnick pressuring you."

He gave me a stern look. Aha! I knew exactly what was coming.

"Chloe, you know I can't — "

" — talk about an active investigation. I knew it!" Strike two.

Now he looked twice as stern. "I'm going to tell you exactly what I told the reporter who wrote that frankly irresponsible story. We are attempting to reconstruct the last few hours of Peter Flosnick's life in order to understand exactly what happened on MacAdam's Lookout on the night in question."

Yup. Something was going on all right.

\* \* \*

Have you ever been in a situation where you're supposed to be concentrating on one thing, but all you can think about is something else, something totally unrelated? Love can do that to you — you're supposed to be studying chemistry, but instead of formulas you see a certain somebody's eyes. Fear can do it, too. You have a big date lined up, maybe a date with Mr. Right, the man of your dreams, and anyone in their right mind would be thinking about that, but first you have to get through a little dental surgery, and, hey, what if the dentist's hand slips and instead of going into your upper jaw, that great big needle glides up through the roof of your mouth right into your eyeball? (Don't tell me you haven't ever been terrified by *that* possibility.) Puzzles can distract you, too.

I had a chemistry test the next day. As a symbol of my good intentions, I had my chemistry textbook open on my bed. But I wasn't studying it. I wasn't even looking at it. Instead, I was staring at something else altogether. It happened like this:

I got home, had dinner, washed the dishes (Phoebe dried), and went up to my room to study. First I cleared everything off my bed. If you're going to study, you have to focus. If you're going to focus, you have to eliminate clutter. Away went the miscellaneous notebooks and study sheets. Away went the rest of my school books. Away went the collection of Edgar Allan Poe short stories I had been reading.

When I picked up the Poe book to move it, something fluttered out of it — the slip of paper Peter had been using as a bookmark. Point of precision: the sales receipt from the flower shop that Peter had been using as a bookmark. I picked it up and was about to crumple it and toss it into my wastebasket — what did I need an old receipt of Peter's for? — when I noticed something scribbled in the corner. Well, not scribbled exactly. More like signed. Initialed, actually. Someone had written their initials at the bottom of the receipt.

I ordered flowers from that same shop a couple of weeks after we moved to East Hastings. Peter wasn't there at the time — from what the man at the funeral said, he had quit working there a few months before. It was the time Levesque had asked me to order flowers for Mom because he was tied up at work.

"Ever heard of the telephone?" I'd asked him. It sounded sarcastic — it was supposed to — so just imagine the look he gave me. "Seriously," I said, "you can order flowers by phone."

"I want them to be nice. I want to see what they look like before I pay for them."

I knew where this was going. "And if you can't see, then you want *me* to see, right?"

Right.

So I was dispatched to the one and only flower shop in town, where I ordered flowers — not just nice flowers, but spectacular flowers; after all, it wasn't *my* money — from the most uptight, fussiest man on the planet. This, I now knew (thanks to Peter's funeral) was the owner of the shop. I told him where I wanted the flowers delivered. He made me repeat the address slowly (and supply a phone number, just in case — in case of what, he didn't say) while he carefully printed the address on a receipt in one of those receipt books filled with that special paper that produces a duplicate receipt without carbon paper. The original went to me, the duplicate stayed in the book.

After he had slowly — agonizingly slowly — taken down the address, he read it back to me, also slowly, glancing up at me after each item — 91 (glance) Hillside Avenue (glance), here in town (glance), not the Hillside Avenue over in Linzey (glance), phone number 555 (glance) 8892 (glance). "I wouldn't want either of us to make a mistake," he said. I said it was unlikely my own address could trip me up. He didn't even crack a smile. "Now then," he said, holding out a pen and turning the receipt book around so that it faced me, "initial here."

"What for?"

"To indicate that this is the address you gave me."

Talk about a compulsion for checking. This guy was borderline obsessive. "You just read it back to me to make sure you'd written it down right."

"You can't be too careful," he said. "I don't want you blaming me if these flowers get sent to the wrong address because you gave me incorrect information."

I opened my mouth to argue. I like a good argument. But I decided this one would probably turn out to be a pain-in-the-neck stupid argument, and suddenly I couldn't be bothered. I initialed the receipt, took my copy and got out of there.

I looked down now at the receipt I had been about to crumple. Whoever had ordered the flowers described on it had apparently gone through the same ridiculous procedure, because there was a set of initials — LA — in the corner of the paper.

LA. Could it possibly be the LA I had in mind?

* * *

I missed a few questions on my chemistry test the next day. I didn't care. Well, I didn't care at that exact moment. Probably when I got the test back and got a better picture of how much damage my distraction had done, I would care a whole lot more. But when the bell rang, all I could think about was dropping my test paper on Mr. Szekula's desk and getting over to Mrs. Flosnick's house as fast as I could.

I started out at a dead run, but drew up short in the school parking lot. There, sitting in what an ordinary person might think was an unmarked police car but what looked to me like the family car, was Levesque. He wasn't alone. He had a man with him, in the passenger seat. A man I had never seen before. Both of them were staring intently at the front door of the school as students started to stream out. I raised a hand to wave to Levesque. He saw me, but only gave me a stern look. Fine. Terrific. Just let him ask me why I never called him Dad. I turned away and saw Thomas sheltered in one of the school's side exits. He was looking at Levesque, too, then he spotted me and nodded toward the car. The gesture looked sort of like a body-language question mark. I shrugged in response — I was probably going to be the last person to know what was going on — and hurried over to Mrs. Flosnick's house.

She was surprised to see me. She was friendly, though, so I guess she didn't hold it against me that Levesque wasn't pursuing the foul-play angle. (Or was he? What was he doing at school? I wondered. And who was that man with him? Did that have something to do with Peter Flosnick, or was he working on another case?)

"What can I do for you, Chloe?" Mrs. Flosnick said.

"I just wanted to see how you were doing," I said. It was a lie. That wasn't what I wanted at all. "And I wanted to thank you for giving me those books of Peter's. I've been reading them."

Her eyes misted over a little at the mention of Peter's name, but her smile remained firmly in place.

"I'm glad," she said.

We looked at each other for a moment. I was hoping she would say something to fill a little of the awkward space between us. She was probably expecting me to do the same, which was too bad because I'm not the kind of person who fakes it well.

"Mrs. Flosnick," I said, "I was wondering . . . I wanted to ask you about your friend Ms. Braden."

"Oh?" She couldn't have sounded more confused if I had suddenly started gabbling at her in Latin.

"She used to live around here, didn't she? Over on Dewhurst?" That was the street name that appeared on the receipt tucked into Peter's book. I was guessing, of course, but it was what you'd call an educated guess.

Mrs. Flosnick nodded.

"Her birthday isn't in March, by any chance?"

"Why, yes, it is. March 12." She peered at me now. "May I ask why you want to know?"

"My birthday's in March, too," I said. Another lie. "I'm a Pisces." Actually, I'm an Aries. "Peter told me once that I reminded him of a friend of his mother's — of yours." Another lie. Maybe I was better than I thought at faking it. "He said Pisces people are all alike — dreamers and romantics. Anyway, I was reading one of his books last night and I started thinking about him and, I don't know, I was just curious to know who he meant when he said that. Stupid, huh?"

She was crying. Mrs. Flosnick was standing there listening to me lie like a natural and she was crying.

"I'm — I'm sorry, Mrs. Flosnick. I didn't mean to upset you."

"I'm not upset," she said. You could have fooled me. "I'm just glad you were thinking about Peter. I'm glad I'm not the only person remembering him."

I suddenly felt terrible. So terrible that I accepted her invitation to tea and followed her into the kitchen and listened to her talk and talk and talk about Peter. To hear her tell it, he didn't seem like such an oddball. In fact, he sounded pretty smart, even if he was obsessed by a passion for stars. But obsession isn't necessarily a bad thing. Where would the ceiling of the Sistine Chapel be if Michelangelo hadn't been obsessed? Where would

146

the light bulb be without Edison's fixation on something everyone else thought was nuts? And what
about the Wright brothers and flight? Peter
Flosnick started to sound like the kind of guy who
might have grown up to be a modern Galileo, a guy
who might one day be famous for all the things he
knew about the night sky, space, our universe, the
galaxies beyond. In one way, I wished I had gotten
to know him better. When I told her that, she started to cry all over again. But this time, she smiled
through her tears and I knew she was going to be
all right.

* * *

LA. Lise Arsenault?

I pieced together the bits I knew, strung them
together with a few — admittedly tentative — sup-
positions, and came up with a reasonable theory.
Maybe it had happened this way: Lise Arsenault,
determined to break up her father's relationship
with Eileen Braden, had gone to the one and only
flower shop in town on March 12, Eileen Braden's
birthday, and had ordered flowers sent to Ms.
Braden's house, enclosing a card guaranteed to
enrage her already jealous father. The man in the
shop, fussy as ever, had taken down the Dewhurst
address and had read it back to Lise, then made
her initial the receipt. Maybe Lise had tossed the
receipt into the wastebasket in the store — she
wouldn't want her father to find the receipt. Maybe
she had discarded it carelessly somewhere else.
The flowers had been delivered, the damage had

been done. And then, maybe the same day, maybe the next day, maybe even later than that, after Paul Arsenault's breakup with Eileen Braden, Peter Flosnick had stumbled across the receipt. He knew Eileen Braden — she was his mother's best friend. He would have recognized the address. He might also have known it was Eileen Braden's birthday. He also knew Lise. If he had heard about the breakup — and from what Eileen Braden herself had said about why she moved to Morrisville, it would have been a miracle if Peter hadn't heard — maybe he had figured out or had guessed what had happened. Maybe he had even been in the shop that day when she had ordered the flowers. Maybe he had seen her sign the receipt.

Problem: If Peter knew, as everyone seemed to, why Paul Arsenault had broken up with Eileen Braden, and if he knew, as I suspected he did, who had ordered the flowers that had precipitated the breakup, why hadn't he told Eileen Braden? She was a friend of the family. A close friend. Why hadn't Peter given her the ammunition she needed to prove to Paul that she hadn't been cheating on him?

Slow down, Chloe. Maybe you're dead wrong. Maybe Peter hadn't understood the significance of the receipt. Maybe it was just a coincidence that he even had it. Maybe Lise had thrown it into the garbage before she left the shop and Peter had picked it up and used it to mark his place in the book he was reading. That had to be it, didn't it? Because if Peter had understood the significance of the receipt with Lise Arsenault's initials on the bottom of it, and if he *hadn't* used that information to help Eileen Braden, then what did that say about him? What kind of person would have kept that information to himself instead of using it to help out a friend? Peter was odd. He was even a little weird. But surely if he had known anything, he would have used what he knew to help Eileen Braden. Surely that was as elementary as ABC.

Have you ever had this happen to you? You're cruising along, having a perfectly good day, and someone says to you something along the lines of, "Remember that movie where the guy's a has-been boxer and he has this evil manager who owes money all over town and he's trying to turn this boxer into a wrestler?" And, sure, you remember it. Then the person says, "What was the name of that movie, anyway?" You've seen the movie. You can picture it clearly — it was in black and white and it starred that fat guy who used to have a TV series way back when, what was his name? Jackie something. Jackie Gleason. Yeah, that's it. You saw the movie and you thought it was pretty good, but, for the life of you, you can't remember the name of it. So it drives you crazy all day. All day you try to come up with the name, and all day you draw a blank.

Then you go to bed.

About four a.m. your eyes pop open and you sit bolt upright in the dark. The name is now flashing before you as if you'd just woken up in front of a neon sign: *Requiem for a Heavyweight*. You lie down, a big smile on your face. All is now right with the world.

As elementary as ABC . . .

AMW, BDD, CLA . . . Minus the ABCs and what do you have? MW, DD, LA, AG.

LA.

Lise Arsenault. Whose name was on the receipt, the receipt in Peter's book. Coincidence? LA. 100-03-15. 100-04-15. 100-05-15.

Lise Arsenault: one hundred . . . One hundred what? Flowers? Roses?

Dollars? Hmm.

And what about 03-15? What was that? A date, maybe? Third day, fifteenth month? No, stupid, there is no fifteenth month. How about third month, fifteenth day? March 15. Double-hmmm. March 15 was three days after Eileen Braden's birthday. Three days after Lise sent Eileen Braden the flowers that torpedoed her relationship with Lise's dad. Which Peter had proof of. And, if that 100 was one hundred dollars, then that would explain why Peter didn't tell. Maybe.

Okay, so if CLA was Lise Arsenault, what about AMW, BDD, and CAG? Matt Walker, Daria Dattillo and . . . And who? And anyway, was I crazy . . . or was I on to something?

# Chapter 13

I was pretty sure that Daria's prize-winning and much-praised poems were stolen from her sister. What if Peter had *proof* that they were? That would explain the DD notations in his book. But what about MW? And who was AG?

Matt Walker had never, so far as I knew, been a friend of Peter Flosnick's. But he had presented himself as one to Peter's mother. He had gone over to Peter's house after the funeral and, on the pretext of sharing Peter's interest in astronomy, had borrowed the videotapes Peter had made of the night sky. I knew he had lied to Mrs. Flosnick. But why? Was he really just curious, as he had told me? Or was there some other reason he wanted Peter's tapes?

I thought about asking Thomas, but Thomas was Matt's best friend. If I started quizzing him, he might tell Matt, even if I made him promise not to. I know I'd tip off my best friend if someone started asking a million questions about him or her, no matter what kind of promise I might have made. I decided to ask Ross Jenkins instead. I found him in the newspaper office.

"What do you know about Matt Walker?" I said.

Ross arched an eyebrow as he looked up at me. "Well, for one thing, I know he already has a girlfriend."

Cute. "I'm not conducting a background check on a potential boyfriend," I said.

"Oh, right." He slapped his forehead, a little too dramatically, if you ask me. "You already have a jock wrapped around your little finger. I forgot."

Okay, I could see this was going to get me nowhere. I turned to leave. Ross caught up with me as I was opening the office door.

"I'm sorry," he said, and looked suitably contrite. "I'm being a jerk."

"I didn't know you were interested in me, Ross." Okay, so I was teasing him, but he really *was* being a jerk.

He tried to look indignant. He might have succeeded, too, if it weren't for the tattle-tale blush on his cheeks.

"Who said I was interested?"

"Oh," I said, all innocence. "You mean there's some other reason you're acting like a jerk?"

Now he turned scarlet — and changed the subject.

"What do you want to know about Matt?"

"What's the dirt on him?"

"Dirt?" He gave me an odd look.

"You're the newspaper editor. You must hear all kinds of good gossip. Are there any rumors circulating about Matt?"

If Ross had been a dog, his ears would have been standing at attention. As it was, they almost were. He was probably dying to know why I was asking such a strange question. He didn't ask, though.

"Nothing I know of," he said. "Other than if anyone ever deserved to have Artie Lambton as a stepfather, it's Matt."

"Why do you say that?"

"Because Artie's an even bigger loser than Matt is. Have you ever talked to the guy? He's always dropping names and quizzing people about how much they paid for things. He loves to boast about how much he spent on his house and his boat and whatever other new toy he's just bought. He always acted like some kind of sleazy used-car salesman, and he's only gotten worse now that he's made a fortune on that development deal of his."

"Clear Meadows, you mean?"

"Yeah. After the mines started struggling a bit, everybody thought he was crazy to build a subdivision. But as Artie kept saying, 'If you build it, they will come.'"

"Well, they have, haven't they?"

Ross nodded grudgingly. "He sold Clear Meadows as the perfect retirement place for people tired of city living," he said.

"So the guy is a super-salesman."

Ross nodded. "He was the only person who succeeded in getting Elizabeth Flosnick to even talk about selling the land Clear Meadows was built on. And she sold it practically over Peter's dead body."

That was interesting. "Peter didn't want her to sell?"

"No way."

"Why not?"

"Peter's family owned that land for generations. I guess after Peter's father died, Peter figured it would be his. He went crazy when his mother sold it, and he went crazier still when Artie started to build on it. I guess in a way I can sympathize with him — who'd want to look out your bedroom window onto an ugly subdivision, especially when you're used to having a clear view of the lake?"

Peter being angry with his mother for selling a piece of land to Artie Lambton didn't explain why Matt's initials — assuming they were Matt's — were in his book.

"Matt wasn't happy when his mother decided to marry Artie, was he?"

"Wasn't happy?" Ross snorted. "He was ready to kill. Figuratively, of course."

"Did he try to break up his mother and Artie?"

Ross nodded. "It's practically the favorite sport in this town — messing up your parents' love lives. Lise and her dad, Matt and his mom."

"Except that Lise succeeded," I pointed out.

He gave me an odd look. "What makes you say that?"

"Her father broke up with Eileen Braden."

"From what I heard, Paul Arsenault was insanely jealous. That's what broke them up."

If that's what he thought, fine. It wasn't relevant.

"Matt hated Artie," Ross continued. "Probably still hates him. You should have seen him the night Artie proposed to Lenore. What a night!"

"What do you mean? What night?"

"The night of the fire. Christmas Eve."

"*You* were with Matt Walker on Christmas Eve?"

I got another shot of Ross's indignation. "What, I'm not in his league, is that what you mean?"

"I mean, I didn't think you liked jocks — " Nice save, even if I do say so myself. " — so I'm surprised you'd hang around with him."

He seemed to accept that. "Half of East Hastings was hanging around with him that night. Well, not with him exactly. With Artie and Lenore — "

I looked puzzled, I guess, so Ross elaborated. "They threw a huge Christmas party. I guess that was because Artie was planning to announce their engagement that night — but nobody knew that at the time. It was a big surprise. Anyway, they invited my parents and because it was Christmas Eve my mom made me go, too. She has this thing about the family being together on Christmas Eve. So I went. Anyway, Matt spent most of the evening lurking in a corner, looking like he was ready to stab Artie through the heart with a shrimp fork. Whenever Artie kissed Lenore or put his arm around her, Matt would glower at him and then leave the room. A couple of times he took off for maybe an hour. What a jerk! Then, around sometime after ten, someone started yelling *fire*. And, boy, what a fire! The whole sky was lit up."

"Clear Meadows?"

Ross nodded. "It was pretty far gone by the time the alarm was sounded. Half of East Hastings was at the party, and Clear Meadows is on the other side of town. I guess no one saw anything until it was too late. By the time the fire department got mobilized, Clear Meadows had half-burned to the ground. Everyone piled into their cars and raced over there, me included. I remember looking through the crowd and seeing Matt. For the first time that night, he was smiling. He kept right on smiling, too, even after we all went back to the party — "

"The party continued after something like that?" I could hardly believe it.

"Artie insisted. He rounded everyone up and brought them back to the party and started pouring champagne. Lenore looked a little dazed. 'No use crying over spilled milk,' Artie said. He got everyone settled down, and then Lenore said, 'Thank goodness for insurance,' and Artie said to everyone, 'That's why I'm marrying this woman. She really saved my bacon.' Boy, did that knock the smile off Matt's face. It even crossed my mind, kind of like a joke, you know, that maybe Matt had burned the place down."

"So what makes you think he didn't do it?"

He gave me another odd look. "Did anyone ever tell you you ask a lot of strange questions?"

I decided to ignore that one. "What makes you think Matt didn't do it?"

"The insurance company investigated the fire. It figured that they would — they had to pay out an awful lot of money on the claim. According to them, the fire was started by somebody leaving a lit cigarette lying around. Some of the houses were unfinished, and kids used to hang around there. Old guys, too. You know, guys who were just passing through on their way to somewhere else. Guys without much money who were always looking for some place free to crash for the night."

"Matt could have started the fire with a lit cigarette," I said. "You said he left the house a couple of times."

Ross laughed. "You can't be serious," he said. "That would be arson." Then he peered at me. "You are serious, aren't you?" He shook his head. "No. I don't buy it. The insurance company investigated and paid the claim. They ruled it accidental. I assume their investigators knew what they were doing."

"Did anyone tell them that Matt had left the party?"

He shrugged. "How should I know?"

"Did *you* tell them?"

"Well, no."

"Why not?"

"First of all, because no one asked me. And second, you're talking about someone deliberately starting a fire. Someone I know. What kind of a guy would do that?"

"Maybe a guy who didn't want his mother marrying Artie Lambton."

Ross shook his head again. "You'd have to *really* want to stop your mom getting married to do something that drastic."

157

I had seen the way Matt looked at his stepfather. I had heard them fighting. It was obvious to me that Matt really wanted Artie Lambton out of his mother's life. Did that make him the kind of person who would do something so drastic? And if it did, had Peter Flosnick somehow stumbled onto the proof?

"AG," I said.

"What?" Ross looked confused, as if I had said something to him in a foreign language.

"What do the initials AG mean to you?"

"Adam Gillette," said a voice behind me. I spun around to face Eric Moore, who looked sheepishly at me. "Sorry," he said. "I wasn't eavesdropping. Well, not intentionally." He reached past me to hand some papers to Ross. "Here's this week's column."

AG. Adam Gillette. The boy who had drowned after falling through the ice.

"Any dirt on him?" I asked Ross.

Ross rolled his eyes. "Here we go again." When Eric looked puzzled, Ross just said, "You don't want to know."

"Sure, I do," Eric said. "Who's looking for dirt on Adam?"

"Is there any?" I asked. "Any nasty rumors?"

"The guy's dead, Chloe," Ross said.

"Why do you want to know?" Eric asked.

"Idle curiosity?" Ross said.

"I heard he wasn't as perfect as everyone makes him out to be," I said. "Is that true?"

Eric laughed. "I'd like to meet the person who said that guy was perfect. He was one of the best football players I ever saw, but apart from that, he was a pain in the neck. He thought pretty highly of himself, if you know what I mean. He was president of his own fan club. All he ever talked about was how he was going to be scouted for a major football scholarship, how he was going to end up playing pro ball, and how everyone else was going to eat his dust."

"True," Ross said. "But those aren't rumors. Those are facts."

"Yeah," Eric said. Then, "There was that buzz about him using steroids, though."

"What buzz?" Ross asked.

Eric gave him a sour look. "Don't you pay any attention to what goes on around here?"

"To the sports beat, you mean? No. That's your job."

"Right, I forgot, big intellectuals like you hit the snooze button whenever sports is mentioned."

"What was the buzz about Adam and steroids?" I asked Eric. Someone had to keep this conversation on track. "What was that all about?"

"Just that he was using them. It's not allowed, you know."

"Of course I know. It's also dangerous," I said. I don't really follow sports, but even I knew about a couple of football players who had died of cancer that was attributed to steroid use. "It *is* true, though? Was Adam using steroids?"

"Far as I know, it was never confirmed. Maybe it was just locker room talk by some jealous teammates. I guess it doesn't matter anymore."

Maybe it did, and maybe it didn't. One thing was sure, though. It sure didn't matter to Adam Gillette.

* * *

The next day was one of those days that, when you look back on it, you wish you could have just slept through the whole thing. I felt like I was being rained on by bad luck. First, I got my chemistry test back and found out that I had done much worse than I'd thought. In fact, I barely passed. Mr. Szekula dropped my test paper onto my desk as if he were disposing of a bag of garbage. "I expected better from you, Chloe," he said.

Then Ms. Peters rejected my newspaper article, an opinion piece I'd written on why life in a big city is much more mind-expanding than life in a small town. In a big city, the population is more diverse, so you get exposed to people, music, food, clothes and ideas from many different cultures. There's more cultural life in a big city, so you can immerse yourself more readily in film or dance, visual arts or live theater. In a small town like East Hastings, I had observed, by contrast, that it was all sports and television. Ms. Peter's main comment was, "I'm sorry you're not happy here, Chloe. But I'm afraid we can't print an attack on East Hastings just because you're having trouble adjusting." She wouldn't budge no matter what I said.

Afterwards Ross took me aside. "Personally, I didn't think your article was so bad," he said. "It was a little one-sided and I didn't agree with most of it, but it was well-written."

"One-sided? It's an opinion piece, Ross. It's supposed to reflect the opinion of the writer, who in this case is me, who believes that small-town life isn't anywhere near as interesting as big-city life."

Ross half-smiled. It looked like he was making his best effort to look friendly, but wasn't quite succeeding. "Some of us, Ms. Peters included, grew up here. Some of us even think life here is pretty interesting in its own way. We also think our minds are as expanded as anyone else's."

"Which is why some of you believe in censorship," I said. Snidely. But, hey, I was angry.

"Ms. Peters thinks, and I agree, that you could be a little more balanced in your approach."

"Dress it up any way you like, Ross, it's still censorship."

Of course, no one in my family had any sympathy for my point of view.

"What do you expect?" Phoebe said. "You're telling them you think they're narrow-minded. Why would anyone be thrilled about reading that?"

"They're censoring me," I pointed out. I don't know why I bothered. No one seemed to hear me.

"You have to get to know people before you start criticizing them for being themselves," my mother said.

"It's hardly the fault of a small community like

East Hastings that there are no major ballet or opera companies in the area," Levesque added. "If you give it a chance, you might even see the advantages of living in a town like East Hastings." Don't even ask me what he meant by that.

"That's not the point," I said.

He looked at me from under his bushy black eyebrows. "Then what is the point?" he asked.

Suddenly I wasn't so sure.

* * *

I was going out with Thomas that night, which promised a little relief from a bad day. I was still in a bad mood, though. Thomas was in a worse mood.

"How about roller-skating?" I said. It was my fourth or fifth suggestion, and I was scraping the bottom of the barrel.

No response.

"Thomas, are you even listening to me?"

He turned to look blankly at me.

"Thanks," I muttered.

"What?"

"We're supposed to be spending time together," I said.

"I'm here, aren't I?"

"Your body is here. But your mind is obviously elsewhere. What's up?"

"Nothing."

"Still worried about Lise?" It wasn't the smartest thing to say, and maybe I said it in a tone that was nastier than it needed to be. Maybe there was even some jealousy mixed in with the nastiness. But he

162

was supposed to be out with me, and here he was, preoccupied with his ex-girlfriend. Again.

An angry look replaced the blank one. "What's that supposed to mean?" he said.

"I thought we were going to do something fun tonight."

"Like make snide comments about someone I care about?"

Boy, did he push the wrong button. "Oh, so you care about her, do you? Then why don't you go over to her house and see what *she's* doing tonight? Maybe she'll be more fun!"

"Maybe I will," he said, and turned away from me. Fine. Let him go. Who wanted to be anywhere near someone who was in such a foul mood? Then, just when I thought he was going to stomp away, he turned and said, "Sorry. I guess I have a few things on my mind."

"No kidding."

"It's not what you think. It's not Lise. It's just . . . I don't know." He let out a huge sigh. "Don't you ever wish your life was different? Don't you ever wish you could be someone else or do something else, that something exciting would happen, or even something dull, as long as it happened someplace else, someplace maybe halfway around the world? I hate it here sometimes. I've spent my whole life up here and I'm more than ready for a change. I want to see something different besides this lake and those woods. I want to meet different people, I don't want to spend my whole life with

Matt and Lise and Daria." He seemed to run out of steam and sighed again, a smaller sigh, and his shoulders slumped. "You know what I mean?"

"Hey, I'm the queen of that country," I said. "I know exactly what you mean." I'd been in the grip of that feeling ever since I'd been forcibly moved from Montreal. "So why don't we go roller-skating? Or take a walk or something?"

He took forever to think it over. You would have thought I'd asked him to marry me or something. Then, finally, he said, "I'm not good company tonight, Chloe. I'm sorry."

He walked me home, though, and kissed me on the cheek. It was what you might call a duty kiss, the kind of kiss you give someone only because you feel obliged to — it's expected of you, but there isn't anything behind it. A pre-dump kiss.

"I'll call you, okay?"

"Sure." Like I'd never heard that line before. "Feel better," I added. A duty sentiment, the kind of thing you say because you feel obliged to.

* * *

I couldn't sleep that night. Everything had gone wrong, from my chemistry test and my article being cut, to my family's support (okay, lack of support) and Thomas's obviously dwindling interest in me.

I lay in the dark, listening while Phoebe got ready for bed, then Mom and Levesque. Finally, when the house was quiet, I flipped on my light and sat up in bed. Chemistry I could fix — all I had

164

to do was study next time and I would improve. So would Mr. Szekula's estimation of me. My article? Well, I hated to admit being wrong, but maybe Ms. Peters had a point. So did Ross. And my Mom and Levesque. Heck, maybe even Phoebe was right this time. An opinion is just that, an opinion. And not every opinion is worth sacrificing trees for. I would try to come up with another subject to tackle.

As for Thomas, maybe he was getting ready to dump me, and maybe he wasn't. Either way, I'd probably survive. It wasn't as if I was planning to marry the guy.

I decided to put the day behind me and focus on something else. So I reached for Peter's copy of the Edgar Allan Poe book and flipped to the pages where Peter had written down all those initials and numbers. I fingered the receipt from the flower shop, proof positive that Peter had known that Lise had sent the flowers that had launched her father's breakup with Eileen Braden. But what about Daria and Matt and Adam? What proof had Peter had of their secret crimes?

Daria had gone to Peter's house looking for a notebook. She hadn't found it. Did that mean that it was still in Peter's possession? It couldn't be, though. Not if Mrs. Flosnick hadn't been able to find it in Peter's room. What had she told me? That she had looked everywhere, through all of Peter's things. Did that mean that the notebook didn't exist? Maybe Peter had destroyed it. Or maybe he had some secret hiding place for it. If he did, then for sure I would never find it. I didn't know Peter well enough to guess where he might hide things, and I didn't know East Hastings well enough to even begin to guess where all of its possible hiding places might be.

I looked down at the book in my hand. Peter had hidden his secret notes in an Edgar Allan Poe book. In the pages of a single Edgar Allan Poe story, to be precise. I stared at the title again. Then, like a fish hooked on a line, I was drawn to the box that I had shoved into the back of my closet. Could it be?

# Chapter 14

There were dozens of pieces of unopened mail in the box Mrs. Flosnick had given to me to return to the newspaper office. No, make that dozens and dozens. Some were regular-sized envelopes, the kind that usually contain letters. Some were big brown envelopes, and most of these were thick. They looked as if they might contain magazines. A couple were small and fat — too small to hold what I was looking for. I picked out all of the big, thick brown ones and opened them one by one.

A magazine.

Another magazine.

A couple of comic books — not Superman or Batman or X-men or anything like that, but comics I had never heard of, black-and-white comics about regular people. I flipped through them and made a note to myself to read them later.

A catalog of telescopes.

Another catalog from a science book club.

Then, finally, a notebook. A thick spiral-bound notebook filled with the same loopy handwriting I had seen on all those sheets of paper stuffed in the bottom drawer of the desk I was using at the newspaper office. Before me, that drawer had belonged to Anna Maria Dattillo, Daria's sister. This must have been the notebook Daria had been looking for.

I turned page after page, scanning the notes and poem fragments and drafts, until I came to some lines that sounded familiar. No wonder. They were the same lines that had appeared in the special two-page spread in the school newspaper that had featured the prize-winning poems of Daria Dattillo. So Peter had known. He had known, and he had told Daria that he knew. If I was right, he had been blackmailing her. Well, well. And, just like the villain in Poe's "The Purloined Letter," he had hidden his proof in plain sight. I wondered how many people had passed by his mailbox in the newspaper office and had never thought much about what it contained.

Peter had hidden his proof of Lise's crime in a similar way. It had been nestled in the Poe book the whole time. I had seen him with the book at school. Probably lots of people had. You had to hand it to Peter, he was one smart guy.

Okay, so that nailed down Lise and Daria. I went over my conversation with Ross about Matt and Artieville. If Matt *had* been behind the fire, and Peter knew . . .

Mrs. Flosnick had told me that Matt had borrowed all of Peter's videotapes. Peter had made those tapes with a video camera attached to the lens of his telescope. They were, Mrs. Flosnick said, tapes of the night sky. But what if, one night, Peter's telescope had been trained on a more terrestrial target? Clear Meadows sprawled between the back of the Flosnick property and the lake.

From his bedroom window, Peter had a good view of the whole development. What if, one night — say, Christmas Eve — he had pointed his telescope at Clear Meadows, and what if he had seen someone lurking there, someone who looked suspicious, someone who might have started a fire? What if he had captured that person and that person's actions on tape? And what if he had used that tape to extort money?

The next morning I headed straight for the newspaper office, which was deserted except for Ross. He spent so much time in that office that I was beginning to think he needed a few other interests in life. He obviously thought that I shared his enthusiasm for the paper because the first thing he said to me was, "Finished that article on the school's foster child yet?"

I hadn't. The truth was, I hadn't even started. "I'll have it in on time," I assured him.

"You know, Chloe, newspapers run on deadlines," he said, as stern as a father or a vice-principal. "If people don't meet their deadlines, it puts pressure on others to fill in for them. That's not fair."

Oh, terrific, I thought. He was taking another kick at me for the failed Daria Dattillo profile, which hadn't even been my fault.

"Relax, Ross," I said. "I promised I'd do it and I will."

He nodded, but anyone reading the look on his face probably would have concluded that I had missed a hundred deadlines so far this year.

"Hey, Ross, about that Christmas party — "

If he had been a computer, his little red processing light would have been blinking. Christmas party, Christmas party . . . Since when were we talking about a Christmas party?

"The one at Matt Walker's place," I prompted. "The one you told me about, when Clear Meadows burned down and Artie proposed to Lenore?"

File found. The little red light stopped flashing.

"Yeah," he said. "What about it?"

"Was Peter there?"

"Flosnick?"

"Yes. Was he at the party that night?"

"You have to be kidding. I think Peter hated Artie Lambton even more than Matt did. If it hadn't been for Artie, Peter's mother never would have sold that land."

"So he wasn't there?"

"I didn't see him . . . No," Ross said finally, "he wasn't there.'

"You're sure?"

"Of course I'm sure. I was there, remember?" He peered at me. "What's going on, Chloe?"

"Nothing." As I went out the door I added, "And don't worry about that article. I'll have it done on time. Promise."

As I hurried to my first class of the day, I thought again about Matt borrowing all of Peter's videotapes. When I had surprised Matt in his basement recreation room just before the concert, he had scrambled to shut off his VCR. Why? Had he found the incriminating tape among Peter's collection? If he had, had he now destroyed it? It was possible, I realized. Maybe it was even probable.

Or was it?

Neither the receipt from the flower shop nor Anna Maria Dattillo's notebook had been hidden where one might have expected. In fact, I had found them in just about the last place a person would have thought to look, not the first. Why, then, would Peter keep his videotape of Matt — assuming there was such a videotape, assuming I wasn't letting my imagination run wild — why would he keep that tape in with the rest of his collection? It was too obvious. It wasn't Peter's style. Wouldn't Peter have hidden that tape someplace else, someplace where Matt would never think of looking?

I went hunting for Matt after school. As it happened, I didn't have to expend much energy on my search. He was on the front steps of the school, draped around Lise like an old sweater, nuzzling her neck. She looked too distracted to be enjoying his attention. Maybe her father was spending more time with Eileen Braden.

"Hi, Matt," I said. Then, only because it would have been flat-out rude not to, I added, "Hi, Lise."

They gave me a pair of brisk get-lost looks.

"I wanted to ask you about those tapes of Peter's you borrowed," I said to Matt.

He didn't react the way I expected. He didn't seem jolted by the question. His face didn't go white from shock or red from discovery. If anything, he seemed bored by the question.

"What about them?" he said.

"I'd like to borrow them."

Lise was the one who registered surprise. "What for?" she wanted to know.

Matt just shrugged. "If you want them, you can have them. I was going to give them back to Mrs. Flosnick, anyway. I'm finished with them."

"Great," I said. If he could be breezy and casual, so could I. "When can I pick them up?"

"What about now?" he said. "I was just heading home."

More surprise from Lise. "You were?"

Matt kissed her on the cheek. "And you were just coming with me, right?"

I climbed into Matt's car with Matt and Lise and we drove to his house. I followed him and Lise downstairs to the recreation room, where Lise curled up on the sofa. Matt handed me a cardboard box full of videotapes.

"You sure they're all there?"

"Yeah, they're all there. Why? You looking for something special?"

"Not really," I said. "Were you?"

He grinned, which was also not what I expected.

"There was nothing to find," he said. "Just a bunch of stars and a lot of black sky. I don't know why Flosnick was always going on about those tapes. There's nothing on them worth looking at. If you ask me, there never was."

I left, clutching the carton of tapes, and didn't set it down until I was well out of sight of the Walker house. Then I counted. Twelve . . . thirteen . . . fourteen. Mrs. Flosnick had said there were fourteen tapes in all, a total of one hundred and twelve hours of viewing pleasure. As far as I could see, they were all present and accounted for. That didn't mean that there wasn't something on one of those tapes that incriminated Matt, though. Maybe there had been, and Matt had found it and erased it. Maybe that explained his smug attitude. Or maybe he was confident that no one would ever have the patience to sit through all fourteen tapes and so would never discover the few minutes that could ruin him. Let's face it, if you're going to settle down to watch more than one hundred hours — four solid days — of scenes of the night sky, you have to be the type of person who doesn't mind sifting a beachful of sand on the off-chance that you'll find one specific grain. You also have to believe that that grain, or that minute or two of incriminating footage, is in there somewhere.

Or maybe Matt's cheerfulness was the result of having gone through the tapes and not finding anything at all. Maybe he had concluded that Peter had been bluffing all this time and that now, with Peter safely out of the way, he had nothing to worry about. If that were true, then maybe I was right, maybe Peter had hidden his tape somewhere less obvious.

This time when I knocked on Mrs. Flosnick's

door, I had a good pretext for being there.

"Matt Walker asked me to return these to you," I said, holding out the box of tapes.

"How nice of you, Chloe," she said. "Come in." She held the door to let me pass. "Can I get you anything? A soda? A cup of tea?"

"A cup of tea would be nice," I said, although, to be honest, I don't particularly like tea.

"You can put that box down right there," she said, pointing to a small table in the front hall. Then, "Please, make yourself comfortable in the living room. I'll just put the kettle on. I won't be a minute."

By the time she joined me, I was examining her collection of videotaped soap operas with great interest.

"You have an amazing collection!" I said. "I bet you have a year's worth of reruns here."

She laughed. "Just Tuesdays and Thursdays, I'm afraid," she said. "Those are my volunteer days at the hospital. If you tried to watch those tapes, you'd find the story line a little jumpy. I don't even know why I hang on to them. It's not likely I'll ever watch them again."

"Still, soap operas move slowly enough that you can follow them even if you only watch every other episode," I said.

In the kitchen, the kettle started to screech. While Mrs. Flosnick hurried off to make the tea, I continued to scan her collection and to read the neat hand-printed labels on the spines of the video boxes. On the lowest shelf, at one end, half-hidden by a plant, I spotted a spine that had been labeled in different handwriting. It looked like the same handwriting on the tapes I had just set down on the little table in the front hall. The label on this particular tape read, "Night of Danger." I was bending to pull it from the shelf when Mrs. Flosnick came back into the room, carrying a tray with teapot, cups, milk and sugar.

"Did you find something you want to watch?" she asked. Then, before I could answer, she said, "Please, feel free to borrow some of them. They're just gathering dust here."

I've always believed that when opportunity knocks, you should open the door. "Really?" I asked, as if she had just offered to lend me the crown jewels of England. "You don't mind?"

"Not at all," she said.

I took the tape that was labeled in Peter's handwriting and two more besides, and stuffed them into my backpack. Then I sat down and drank tea with Mrs. Flosnick and we discussed the plotline of her favorite soap opera as if we were discussing the goings-on of friends and neighbors who were plagued by alarmingly bad luck.

That night I waited until everyone in the house was asleep. Then I crept downstairs and slipped "Night of Danger" into the VCR. It made for very interesting viewing.

# Chapter 15

I meant to get up early the next morning to tell Levesque what I had found out. Two things went wrong with that plan, though. First, I overslept. In fact, I probably wouldn't have gotten out of bed at all if Phoebe hadn't come hammering on my bedroom door, demanding to know if I had stolen her new jeans. I hadn't. Second, by the time I hauled myself out of bed, Levesque was long gone.

"He has an all-day meeting," my mother told me.

"At the police station?"

"At the municipal building."

"What kind of meeting?" When I thought about Levesque and work, I thought about crime and punishment. I sure didn't think about meetings.

"A regional administrative meeting," Mom said with a sigh. "I think it has something to do with the police budget."

Okay. It wasn't the end of the world. So far as I could tell, no one suspected what I knew. My little talk with Levesque would have to wait until later in the day.

It's a good thing none of my teachers decided to spring a surprise test on us that day, because I would have failed for sure. I kept thinking about Daria and Lise and Matt. I wanted to tell someone what I had found out. I wanted someone to tell me that maybe I really was on to something. I hoped someone would eventually be able to tell Mrs. Flosnick that she was right, that Peter *hadn't* taken his own life.

I got home a little before Levesque and I staked out the front hall, waiting to hear the tires of his car crunch up the gravel of our driveway. I couldn't wait to run through my deductive reasoning with him. When I finally did hear tires, I rushed to the door to greet him. I even spit out the first few words. "About Peter Flosnick . . . "

That's as far as I got. He cut me short with a withering look.

"Whatever it is, I don't want to hear it," he said. No, not said. Barked. Like a dog barking at some pesky little kid who was harassing it. Like I deserved to be shut down before I had even told him what was on my mind. Like, how dare I bother him!

"Tough day?" my mother said, all sympathy — for him. She had known me for — what? — almost nine times longer than she had known him, but hey, don't let a sense of loyalty to your own daughter stand between you and your man, Mom. I headed for the front door. Levesque blocked my path.

"I'm sorry I snapped at you, Chloe," he said. "But — "

If you ask me, any apology that starts with "Sorry, but . . . " isn't an apology at all. It's a justification. It's not my fault I'm in a lousy mood. Well, I was in no mood to listen to someone tell me why he thought he was perfectly within his rights to snarl at me.

"Whatever it is, I don't want to hear it," I snapped.

"Chloe — "

I pushed by him out the door, and didn't turn back even when I heard my mother call, "But supper is almost ready."

* * *

I thought I didn't know where I was going. I thought I was just getting as far from my house as possible. But if I didn't know where I was going, how come I ended up across the street from Thomas Rennie's house, watching him drag a couple of garbage cans from the back of his house to the curb? He saw me after he had wrestled the second mammoth can into place.

"Hey, what's up?" he said.

"Just wanted to see how you're doing," I said. "You seemed a little, well, distracted the last time I saw you." Talk about an understatement! And the distraction had been Lise, of all things. I don't claim to know everything there is to know about boy-girl relationships, but I do know that when a guy is spending time with one girl while at the same time worrying about *another* girl — his ex-girlfriend, no less — it's a good sign that he's circling around the idea of dumping the first girl. Which, in this case, was me.

Thomas smiled, but it didn't hide his obvious discomfort.

"I guess I was in a pretty lousy mood, huh?" he said, and ducked his head a little. When he did that, he reminded me of a little boy who had been caught sneaking candy before supper and who was trying to charm his way out of a scolding. And I fell for it. I thought, okay, so maybe he wasn't about to dump me after all. Maybe things had been just as he had said — he had been in a bad mood, he was impatient to grow up and get out of town. We stood on the street for a few moments looking at each other and then looking away from each other, both trying to appear casual (at least, that's was what I was trying to do). Then he said, "You want to go for a walk or something?"

We strolled down his street and away from the center of town, toward the lake.

"Thomas?"

He looked over at me. I hesitated. Lise was his former girlfriend. Matt was his best friend. He had known Daria for years. Do you think, I had been going to ask him, do you think any of those three could have pushed Peter Flosnick over the edge of MacAdam's Lookout?

Just forming the question — what seemed like such an absurd question — made me stop. Yes, I had uncovered three people who, it could be argued, had a motive for wanting to get rid of Peter Flosnick. Three people he was possibly blackmailing. Three people who were maybe finding their predicament unbearable, who were maybe ready to crack under the strain of someone holding some-

179

thing over them. So, tell me, Thomas, you've known these people for much longer than I have. Which one of them do you think might have killed Peter Flosnick? It sounded crazy no matter how I tried to put it into words. Things like this didn't really happen, did they? But if they didn't, why was this particular puzzle starting to come together in the shape of "Yes, they did?"

Thomas looked expectantly at me. He smiled and slipped an arm around my shoulder, then leaned down and kissed me on the cheek.

"I'm sorry about the other day," he said. "I don't know what came over me. I guess I was just worried."

"Worried about what?"

He kept his arm around me, but looked away.

"I saw your stepfather at school the other day. He had some guy in the car with him. They seemed to be looking for someone. Any idea what that was all about?"

I shook my head. "He never tells me anything."

"Do you think you could find out?" he asked. His eyes rested so lightly on me that all I could think was, he doesn't want to dump me at all. He never wanted to dump me. And maybe he hadn't been thinking about Lise at all the other day. Maybe there had been something else going on. Maybe it was exactly what he had said, maybe it was just restlessness — nothing to do with me. "Can you ask your stepdad?"

"I can ask," I said, "but I won't get anything out

of him." When he looked disappointed, I added, "You don't know him. He's a by-the-book kind of guy. Work is work. He doesn't discuss it with civilians."

"So that must mean that he *was* looking for someone," Thomas said. "Do you think it had anything to do with Flosnick?"

I shrugged.

Then Thomas said, "You don't think he was looking for Lise, do you?"

Hmmm. Another case of opportunity knocking? Thomas's question made it pretty clear who he would have pointed out if I'd put his three friends in a police lineup and asked him to pick out the guilty one. It also led to an obvious question from me in return.

"Why would he be looking for Lise?" I said.

Thomas gave me the kind of look you usually reserve for the one poor soul who, after the big punch line has been delivered, still doesn't get the joke.

"I heard that someone was seen leaving the park late the night Peter Flosnick died," he said. "I figured maybe the guy who was in the car with your stepfather was the person who had seen something. So then I figured maybe your stepfather brought the guy to school to see if he could recognize anyone." He peered hard at me when I still looked baffled. "Didn't you know?" He sounded surprised to be asking the question.

I shook my head. "How did *you* know?"

It was like asking a juggler how he managed to keep all those balls in the air. He just shrugged. "It's going around," he said. "I thought everyone knew. Peter didn't jump, did he, Chloe? He was pushed. Don't you have any idea who they think did it?"

I shook my head again. "Do you?" I asked. I wanted to hear him say Lise's name again. I wanted him to confirm it.

We had reached the lake. Thomas detached himself from me and scrambled over the rock outcropping to the sandy shore beyond. I felt like a mountain goat as I struggled to stay with him.

"Thomas, do you have any idea who might have pushed Peter — assuming he *was* pushed?"

The look he gave me was one of pure anguish.

"I don't know for sure," he said. "But I've been having this terrible thought. What if it was Lise?"

There it was. I stared at Thomas, trying to digest what he had just said. "You think Lise pushed Peter?"

"I don't know," he said.

"But you just said — "

"She hated Peter."

"From what I've heard and seen, Peter wasn't in danger of winning any popularity contests at school."

"You don't get it," Thomas said. "Lise didn't just think he was a geek. She really disliked the guy. She bad-mouthed him all the time. You should have seen the way she looked at him."

182

"It's a big leap — " I winced at the unintended pun " — from dirty looks to pushing a guy off a cliff."

"What if he was blackmailing her or something?"

I could have said something like, what a coincidence, I was just thinking that myself! But we were talking about his ex-girlfriend, someone he had known a long time, someone he was worried about and, therefore, someone he still obviously cared for a lot. Maybe he was sounding me out, trying to find out from me what the police knew, so that he could warn Lise.

I played it cool. "I don't know, Thomas. That sounds pretty far-fetched."

"I thought so, too, at first," he said. "But remember what I told you about Lise breaking up her father and Eileen Braden? What if Peter knew about that? He worked in the flower shop. Maybe he knew Lise was the one who sent those flowers to Ms. Braden. Maybe he even knew about that tape Lise had me make for her. Maybe he threatened to tell her father about it."

"Even if you're right," I said, "and I'm not saying I agree with you, it still sounds pretty far-fetched to me — " The more I thought about it, the crazier it actually did sound. Who would *kill* someone over flowers and a broken relationship? Or in Daria's case, over some poems written by a dead girl? It was possible, I guess. But probable? No, to be honest, my money was on Matt. Insurance companies don't take arson lightly. If the company that had insured Clear Meadows ever saw the tape that

Peter had made, they'd be suing in a minute to get back all the money they had paid out after the fire. Matt would be in the biggest trouble of his life.

"You don't understand," Thomas said.

"What? What don't I understand?" Did he know about Matt, too? Was he going to tell me about that?

He didn't. Instead, he dropped a bomb on me.

"I saw Lise that night, too," he said.

"What?"

"I was out for a walk that night. I headed down around the lake, then up to the park like I usually do." He nodded toward the southern boundary of the park not more than a few miles away. "I saw a guy walking his dog."

"The same guy Levesque had in his car?"

He shook his head. "I don't know. I didn't get a good look at him. Didn't pay attention, to tell you the truth. Why should I? He was a guy with a dog. I don't even think he noticed me. Then I saw Lise. She was rushing down the path, out of the park."

"Did you talk to her?"

"She was going in the other direction, really fast. I was going to call her. Then I thought maybe she'd had a fight with Matt or something, and if she had, I didn't want to hear about it. It's tough, you know, when your ex-girlfriend is going out with your best friend. You care about them. You really do. But you don't necessarily want to hear every detail, you know what I mean?"

I could imagine.

"What should I do, Chloe?"

"What do you mean?"

"Should I tell your stepfather what I saw?"

"I don't know, Thomas." What I really wanted to say was, no, don't tell. Don't tell because Lise didn't do it. Matt did it. It had to have been Matt. Maybe Thomas didn't know that. Or maybe he did know and he was protecting his friend. Either way, going to Levesque and telling him about Lise was only going to complicate things. At least, Thomas going to Levesque would complicate things.

"Why don't you let me talk to him?" I said at last.

"Would you?"

I nodded. Then I stayed out with Thomas, walking, talking, holding hands, for as long as I dared. When I got home, Mom and Levesque were sitting up waiting for me. The minute I stepped through the front door I saw them, Levesque sitting in the big, over-stuffed armchair in the living room, the reading light over his head trained on a book that lay open in his lap, Mom sitting on the edge of the sofa. She stood up as soon as I came in.

"Where have you been?" she demanded.

"Out," I said, before turning for the stairs.

"Don't you walk away from me, young lady," my mother said in a shrill voice. She sounded angry. "We were worried about you."

"I'm fine," I said. I wasn't being any more reasonable than she was.

"Now, Chloe — " Levesque began.

Mom interrupted him. "You were rude," she told

me. "You were rude to your stepfather and you were rude to me. I'm not going to stand for that, do you understand?"

I glowered at her. Behind her, Levesque sat silent. I knew what he was thinking — it's her daughter, it's up to her to deal with this situation. Fine. Just fine. I turned, ran up the stairs and slammed the door. I sat in the dark, so that they'd think I was asleep. I didn't want either of them coming into my room. How does that kids' song go? *If wishes were horses* . . . A few minutes later I heard footsteps on the stairs, then a knock on my door.

"Go away," I said.

The door opened a crack, instead.

"Is everything okay?" It was Levesque. Finally he had found his voice.

"Fine," I said curtly.

"Look, about the way I snapped at you earlier — I'm sorry, okay? I had a bad day."

It was dark in my room, and what little light could have come in through the door was blocked by Levesque's huge body. I couldn't make out the look on his face. Maybe that would make it easier. I took a deep breath.

"That guy who said he saw someone come out of the park . . ." I began.

I heard a sigh. "Chloe, you know I can't — "

"Which exit?" I asked. "That's all I want to know."

"Why?"

"Which exit?"

Silence.

"Please?" I said.

Another sigh, then, "You're not going to do anything stupid, are you, Chloe?"

"I just need to know," I said.

More silence. Then, miraculously, "Forty Sideroad."

I thought about that for a moment. I also thought about why he had told me. "Apology accepted," I said.

After he closed my door, I turned on the light. I couldn't sleep. I was still angry with my mother, who hadn't come to apologize. And I kept thinking about what Thomas had said. He had seen Lise leaving the park the night that Peter Flosnick died. He hadn't told this to anyone except me. And what he told me was, I think Lise might have killed Peter. Peter worked in the flower shop. Maybe he knew Lise was the one who sent those flowers. Maybe Peter even knew about the tape I made for her.

Did he? Did Peter have a copy of that tape?

I thought again of the box of mail in my closet. I had opened all of the big envelopes when I was looking for Anna Maria Dattillo's notebook. But I hadn't opened any of the smaller packages. I slipped out of bed, retrieved the box, and rummaged through it until I found them. There were four in all, and I opened them one by one. Three contained photographs that people had sent Peter, photographs of the stars. The fourth contained an audiotape, neatly labeled with the initials TR.

Thomas Rennie?

I hunted for my Walkman, found it in a desk drawer, and popped the tape into it. I put on the headphones and pushed the Play button.

The tape didn't contain what I expected — Thomas supposedly making loverboy phone calls to Eileen Braden. Instead, I listened to someone, breathless, making an emergency phone call. "Someone has fallen through the ice at the bottom of Dundas Street," he said. It definitely wasn't Thomas's voice. In fact, if I'd had to put money on it, I would have bet it was Peter talking. "Someone has fallen through the ice and I think he's in trouble. Hurry. Hurry!" The other voice on the tape, the police or the ambulance dispatcher, I wasn't sure which, calmly elicited information from Peter. "Where exactly are you? Where is the person who fell through the ice? Don't go out on the lake, it's too dangerous. Do not, repeat, do *not* attempt a rescue, it's *far* too dangerous. We'll get someone over there right away." Then nothing but some heavy, anxious breathing. Then nothing at all.

I rewound the tape. Before the phone call, I heard a voice, the same voice — Peter's — speaking on the tape. Talking about meteor showers. Between sentences, I kept hearing the click-chonk of the tape recorder being switched on and off. It sounded like Peter had been making notes for an article or maybe a science paper. Then, abruptly, the notes stopped and there was silence. Then I heard a crunching sound, like boots running on snow, and something that sounded like panting. Then the phone call.

I listened to that call three times. Peter had obviously seen someone fall through the ice. But who? Adam Gillette? Maybe. But why did Peter have a tape of this call? Why had he hidden it in the same way he had hidden Anna Maria Dattillo's notebook? And why were the initials TR on the tape?

\* \* \*

The next day at school, I made like a letter carrier. One for you . . . One for you . . . Until my backpack was empty.

The next evening, Mom was working the five-until-closing shift. Phoebe was busy with a school project at the house of one of her new best friends. Levesque was supposed to be home by five-thirty, which would have been perfect, except that at a quarter to six, he still hadn't shown up. Desperate, I called the station house.

"He had a stop to make at the municipal building," said the officer who answered the phone. "But he's going straight home after that, Chloe. He told me so himself."

Shoot! Levesque was a key part of what I had planned. But I couldn't wait. I scribbled a note to him, stuck it to the fridge with a pineapple-shaped magnet and hurried off to my rendezvous.

# Chapter 16

As I waited on MacAdam's Lookout, not too close to the edge, I felt the way I imagined a sleuth in an Agatha Christie book — Hercule Poirot or Miss Marple — might feel when they're close to the big solution. Or, rather, the way they might feel if they were real people.

Daria was the first to arrive. She clutched a small piece of notepaper in her hand. I recognized it as the one I had folded and taped to her locker right after biology class, on my way to the school library for my free period.

"Well, here I am," she said. "What do you want? Why do you think I'd be interested in anything you have to say about Peter Flosnick?"

"You must be," I said, "otherwise you wouldn't be here, would you?" She flashed me a decidedly un-poetic look. "Why don't we wait for the others to arrive?" I said. "That way I'll only have to explain it once."

"Others?" She frowned. "What others?"

As if on cue, Matt sauntered into view. He grinned at me as if something enormously amusing had just happened or was about to happen. Then he glanced at Daria. Neither of them spoke.

Lise was the next to arrive. "I don't know what this is about," she said, waving the piece of paper I had left on her locker, "but I don't know anything about Peter Flosnick and I don't want to know anything."

"Then why did you come?" I asked.

She opened her mouth to answer, then looked angrily at Daria and Matt. "What's going on?" she said.

Matt shrugged.

"Don't worry. I'll explain," I promised.

Thomas was the last to arrive. Like Matt, he seemed calm and relaxed. Of the four of them, he was the only one who'd talked to me about the possibility that Peter's death might not be suicide. He must have suspected why I had called this meeting, but it was obvious he wasn't taking it seriously. That bothered me a lot.

"What's up?" he asked.

"You're probably wondering why I called you all here," I began. It was kind of a joke, a very small one. I don't even know why I said it, because if I was right, this wasn't going to be even remotely funny.

"Your note says you have some information about Peter Flosnick that would interest me," Matt said. "I assume you think it'll interest all of us. So why don't you just get to the point?"

No problem. "I don't think Peter jumped," I said. "I think he was pushed."

Daria let out a little yelp. Everyone looked at her.

"Jumped or pushed, what does it have to do with me, with any of us?" Lise said. "I didn't have anything to do with Peter. I didn't even like him. None of us did."

"I'm sure none of you liked him," I said. "But I'm not so sure none of you had nothing to do with him. I found something interesting in Peter's things." I reached into my backpack and pulled out the Edgar Allan Poe book.

"You found . . . a book?" Matt said. He shook his head, the way people do when someone starts acting crazy. "Fascinating."

"The interesting thing isn't the book itself," I said. "The interesting thing is the notes Peter made in the margins of the book."

"Notes?" Lise said. "What notes?"

"Actually, it's more like a record. A record of his blackmailing activities," I said. "Names, dates, amounts. It's all here."

Suddenly Matt wasn't smirking anymore. "What?" he said. His shock sounded almost convincing. "Are you saying that Peter was blackmailing someone?"

I glared at him, then turned to Lise instead. "Yes, he was. Wasn't he, Lise?"

The rest of them turned to stare at her, too.

"I don't know what she's talking about," she said to her friends. "She doesn't like me. She's making this up."

"Really?" I said. I turned to the page where her initials appeared and read out the notes. "Judging from these dates, I'd say that Peter found out how you sabotaged your father's relationship with

Eileen Braden. He had proof."

"You're crazy."

"Peter had proof that you were the one who sent Eileen Braden those flowers on her birthday," I said. "That was the last straw for your father, wasn't it, Lise? It was the final piece of evidence in your father's mind that Eileen was cheating on him. You torpedoed his relationship with Eileen Braden because you didn't want anyone taking your mother's place, didn't you? Did you think there was still a chance that your parents would get back together? Is that why you've been so upset about your father seeing Eileen Braden again now? Your mother's coming for a visit in a couple of months, isn't she?"

Lise stared silently at me.

"And what would your father have thought if he'd found out what you did? I bet you're afraid he wouldn't be able to forgive you. That's why you went crazy when you saw your father and Eileen together in Morrisville, isn't it? I bet after Peter died you thought you had nothing to worry about. But when your father started spending time with Eileen Braden again, you got worried. You were afraid he might find out that she had never been involved with her bridge partner. He might figure out what really happened, and then you'd have been in big trouble."

"I don't know what you're talking about," Lise said.

"Peter had a receipt from the flower shop, a

receipt for the flowers that were sent to Eileen Braden's house on her birthday. Your initials are on the receipt, Lise. I know. I've seen them. I have the receipt."

Daria and Matt seemed to be following my narrative with apparent fascination. That's when it dawned on me that they hadn't known about any of this. Thomas had, but they hadn't.

Lise stared at me for a very long time before she said, "So what? So what if Peter was blackmailing me?"

"You were in the park the night he died," I said. "Someone saw you."

Her face turned as white as milk. "You think I killed him?" she said. "Is that what this is all about?"

"You were here, weren't you?"

She pulled herself up as tall as she could, like a cat raising its tail and arching its back to make itself appear as large as possible to an enemy. "So what if I was?"

"Did you always meet him here?"

"He loved the cloak-and-dagger stuff," Lise said. "It was like he thought he was some big-time crime king or something. He would tell me to meet him here, always late at night, always at ten o'clock. He would always be sitting on that rock when I arrived. Sitting there and grinning that stupid grin of his. It made me want to — "

"Push him over the cliff?" I asked.

"I didn't kill him."

Eeny, meeny . . .

I turned to Daria.

"I found the notebook," I told her.

She reacted as if I had punched her hard in the stomach, knocking all the air out of her. She groped behind herself for a rock, and lowered herself onto it.

"What notebook?" Matt asked.

"A notebook that belonged to Anna Maria. A notebook full of poems she wrote before she died. You stole them, didn't you, Daria? You stole your sister's poems and passed them off as your own. And Peter found out."

"You ripped off your own sister?" Lise said. She shook her head in disbelief.

"I . . . I didn't mean to," Daria said.

"You didn't mean to put your name on your sister's poems?" Matt said. "Did you do it in your sleep or something?"

Tears trickled down Daria's cheeks. It was a few moments before she could pull herself together enough to speak.

"When Ms. Peters gave us that poetry assignment last year, I didn't know what to do. I can't write poetry. But she expected so much. 'You're Anna Maria's sister,' she said, 'and Anna Maria was so creative, so artistic.'" She paused and wiped at her tears with the back of her hand. "I found Anna Maria's notebook in her room — she had hidden it in a special place in the back of her closet that my parents didn't even know about. I found it and I copied one of the poems and handed it in. Ms. Peters loved it. She showed it to my parents, and they were thrilled. They said it reminded them of Anna Maria and it made them so happy." Now she was really crying. "They — they took Anna Maria's death so hard, you know?" She looked at Lise, as if pleading for understanding. Lise sat down on the rock beside her and slipped an arm around her shoulder.

"My parents thought about Anna Maria all the time," Daria whispered. "My mother cried every day, and my dad kept taking long walks by himself. They didn't talk for months after the accident, not even to each other. But that one stupid poem got them talking again. It even made them smile. Then Ms. Peters wanted me to write more, and my mother encouraged me." She looked up. "I would have stolen a thousand poems to make my mother smile again."

I had been wondering why she'd done it. I thought maybe she had been trying to outshine her sister. Now that I knew the real reason, I felt sorry for her. Sure, you could call her a thief, but she hadn't meant any real harm when she had used her sister's poem. And I knew from firsthand experience how hard it could be to stand up to Ms. Peters once she was on a roll. The whole thing had kind of snowballed out of control.

"Peter found out what I had done," Daria continued quietly. "He threatened to tell. I didn't care about Ms. Peters, but if my parents had ever found out . . . " Her voice trailed off. Then, with quiet frustration, she said, "I don't even know how Peter figured out that the poems weren't mine."

"Probably the same way I did," I said. "He probably saw some of the notes Anna Maria left in her desk at the newspaper office, and he put two and two together."

"All I know is that one day I went to my locker and the notebook was gone," Daria said. "Peter eventually gave me back a photocopy of the book. But he kept the original and he started to blackmail me."

I almost hated to ask the next question, but I had to. When you're sorting out something like this, you have to establish all the facts.

"You were in the park the night Peter died, too, weren't you, Daria?"

She nodded. "But I didn't . . . kill him." She was barely able to say the word.

"What time did you meet him?" I asked.

"Nine-fifteen."

"Did you always meet him at that time?"

She nodded again. "It was always the same. I got here at nine-fifteen, I paid him, then I left. He always made me come in the long way. It gave me the creeps."

"That's because he was a creep," Matt said. "I can't believe you two let that little jerk get to you."

"Are you saying he didn't get to *you*, Matt?" I said.

"Me?" I had to hand it to him. He still looked

relaxed. "You're barking up the wrong tree. Peter didn't have anything on me."

"Are you sure about that?"

If he had been a rooster, he would have been crowing. He acted sure. He acted so sure.

"I'm not stupid," he said. "I didn't send flowers to my father's girlfriend and I sure didn't steal any poems from my sister."

"Like you even have a father or a sister," Lise snorted.

"All you have is a stepfather you could happily live without, right?" I said.

"That's right. Have. As in, still have. I didn't bust up my mother and Artie." I've never seen anyone so smug about failing at his mission in life.

"But you tried to, didn't you, Matt?" I said.

"You've got nothing on me."

So very smug.

I dug into my purse again and brought out the neatly labeled videotape cover. "I guess you haven't seen this one, have you?" I said. "It's a terrific little indie film called *Night of Danger*. It's the tape you were looking for when you borrowed Peter's collection. Too bad for you, though, it wasn't in Peter's collection."

He must have thought I was bluffing because, like Lise, he said, "I don't know what you're talking about."

"I'm talking about arson."

His friends stared at him with drooping jaws. Even Thomas looked surprised. At least, I think it

198

was surprise on his face. Maybe it was something else.

"The fire in Clear Meadows last Christmas was no accident. It was deliberately set," I said. "Peter had a direct view of Clear Meadows from his bedroom window. He also had a powerful telescope. He saw who set the fire. He saw you that night, Matt. He saw you and he taped you. Smile, you're on *Candid Camera*."

Matt dove for the tape cover and wrenched it from my hand.

"Go ahead," I said. "Destroy it. It's just the cover. I have the tape at home."

"What are you planning to do with it?" he asked.

"Yeah," Lise chimed in. "Are you planning to take over from Peter? Become the new local extortionist?"

"She wouldn't do that," Thomas said. "Would you, Chloe?"

I turned and looked into his beautiful blue eyes. How I loved those eyes . . .

"I almost missed you," I said.

He laughed. "What do you mean? I'm right here."

I sighed and glanced at Lise. "Thomas told me what you did," I said. She shook her head, but the way she stared at Thomas, her eyes all wide and filled with hurt and betrayal, I knew she believed me. "He also told me what he overheard about the flowers you had sent to Eileen Braden. If he hadn't, I don't think I would have figured this out."

She kept shaking her head, like someone trying

to wake up from a bad dream. "I trusted you, Thomas," she said.

I just bet she did.

"Oh, and one other thing, Lise," I said. "Thomas said he saw you leaving the park the night Peter died."

Lise was as still as death for a moment. Then her hand flew out so fast it was a blur. The sound it made when it slapped Thomas's face resounded in the little clearing where we stood.

"Hey!" Thomas rubbed his cheek, but that didn't stop a perfect red hand mark from appearing on it. "Hey, I didn't do anything," he said. "I wasn't the one who played a rotten trick on your old man. That was you. You did something wrong and you got caught."

Brief, self-righteous and to the point. Except for one thing.

"I almost missed you," I said to Thomas, "because Peter wrote all of his notes in one place, in 'The Purloined Letter.'"

"In the what?" Matt asked.

"'The Purloined Letter,'" Daria said. "It's the name of a short story by Poe." Maybe she wasn't much of a poet, but she sure did know her Edgar Allan.

"*Your* initials turned up in 'The Telltale Heart,'" I told him.

Everyone turned to stare at Thomas. Thomas ignored them all and looked coolly at me. Those beautiful blue eyes of his were like ice.

"Are you saying he was blackmailing me, too?" he said. "Because if you are — "

"What happened?" I asked him. "Did you lure him out there? Did you tell him it was safe? Or did you just get lucky and he blundered out there on his own?"

"Lure who?" Matt said. "Out where?"

"Adam Gillette," I said, without taking my eyes off Thomas. "Out on the lake just after the thaw."

Thomas didn't flinch, or say a word.

"He was a city kid, like me, wasn't he?" I said. "He was used to skating on rinks. He didn't know anything about lake ice and when it was safe and when it wasn't. But you did, Thomas. You knew, and you didn't warn him."

"Thomas, did you — ?" Lise said.

"I don't know what she's talking about," Thomas said.

You had to hand it to him. He didn't intimidate easily. He didn't even look perturbed. He just stood there, looking convincingly puzzled. He wasn't going to fold until he saw my cards. Maybe he thought I was bluffing. Even though I wasn't, his calm threw me. I began to wish that I hadn't left home in such a hurry.

I reached into my bag and pulled out an audio cassette. "See this?" I said. "Those are your initials. TR."

He looked blankly at the cassette.

"What's on it?" Matt asked. "Thomas Rennie's greatest hits?"

Very funny. "It's a recording of an emergency call Peter made when Adam Gillette fell through the ice."

"I thought they never found out who made that call," Daria said.

"They didn't. But it was Peter, and this tape proves it."

"Why didn't Peter tell anyone it was him?" Lise asked.

"For the same reason he didn't tell the insurance company what Matt did," I said, "or Daria's parents what she did, or your father what you did."

At first I had thought Peter's blackmailing was motivated by money. But that wasn't it. Peter wasn't in it for the money. He had plenty of that, especially after his mother sold that piece of land to Artie Lambton. "All of you treated Peter like garbage. I don't think he appreciated it."

"Maybe we did," Thomas said. "But so what? A recording of Peter making a phone call, even an emergency call, has nothing to do with me — unless he happened to mention my name. Did he?"

He had me there.

"No, he didn't."

Thomas's whole body relaxed into a slouch. "So what makes you think I care anything about that tape and what Peter did or didn't do with it?" he said.

I glanced around for a resting place. There were plenty of them on MacAdam's Lookout. Plenty of rock outcroppings a person could rest on.

"I'm going to tell you what happened," I said. "Then you can tell me whether I'm wrong." It was funny how eyes that had been so warm could turn so cold. "You and Adam were out skating on the lake. Adam was a pretty competitive guy, wasn't he? He was always trying to prove how he was better than you, faster than you, smarter than you, more likely to get that scholarship than you were. Was that what it was all about, Thomas? The scholarship? Eric Moore told me only one of you was going to be offered it."

Nothing. At least, nothing from Thomas. Matt was looking at his best friend with new, horrible interest.

"Did he challenge you, Thomas?" I continued. "Did he say something like, 'Bet I can race you out to the marker. Come on, sucker, let's see who's fastest?' Something like that?" I expected, and got, no answer. "Did he get out in front of you because he was faster or because you let him? Which was it, Thomas?"

Again he didn't answer.

"He went out too far, didn't he, Thomas? But you didn't. You stopped. When Adam went through the ice, you were way back where it was safe. And you didn't do anything to help him. You didn't try to reach him and you didn't head for shore. You just let him scramble in the cold, then you watched him go under. Then you just disappeared. You didn't stop to call anyone. You didn't tell anyone you had been out on the ice. You didn't say a thing."

Three pairs of eyes shifted from me to Thomas.

"You should consider a career as a fiction writer," Thomas said. "You have a great imagination."

"This is one story I couldn't publish without being guilty of plagiarism," I said. I reached into my bag again and this time I pulled out an envelope, which I opened. I removed several sheets of paper from it and held them up so that Thomas could see them. "Peter wrote this," I said. "It's his account of what he saw before he made that emergency call. It's funny, in a way, because at first Peter didn't know who was out on the ice — you were too far out for him to identify you. He didn't even know that he had the emergency call on tape. He was walking along with his tape recorder, making some kind of notes, when he saw Adam go in. When he ran for the phone, he forgot to shut off the tape recorder. But he did have it on tape, which proves he was there and saw what happened. The tape and the letter prove that you were there, too, Thomas."

Thomas's face didn't change. He looked like he was chiseled out of stone. I wondered about his heart, and what that was made of.

"You know what I think, Thomas?" I continued. "I think keeping quiet about what Lise did was one thing. She didn't hurt anyone, at least not physically. But keeping quiet about what you did at the lake, that was something else. Someone died, Thomas. Someone died, maybe because you lured him to it, certainly because you didn't do anything to help him once he was in trouble. It was as good as murder. Peter told you he was going to turn you in, didn't he? He had everything written down in this letter and he was going to hand it over to the police."

"You were out on the lake with Adam?" Lise said to him. She shook her head the way people do when they can't bring themselves to believe something.

"You let Adam die, you killed Peter, and you were ready to sacrifice Lise, isn't that right? When you heard that the police were still looking into the circumstances surrounding Peter's death, you panicked and told me about Lise so that I would tell my stepdad, and he would think she did it."

Lise looked like she wanted to do more than slap him this time.

"Did you tell Thomas you were being blackmailed?" I asked her.

She shook her head. "I didn't tell anyone."

"It makes you wonder how Thomas knew, doesn't it?" I said. "Because he did know, Lise. He told me he thought you were being blackmailed and he told me he saw you leaving the park." I turned back to Thomas. "There's a problem with that, though."

"With what?" Matt asked. Matt, not Thomas.

"Thomas said he was outside the park when he saw a man with a dog. He told me he saw the man near the southern entrance to the park."

Lise frowned. "But I didn't leave by the — "

"I know," I said. "The man who saw you said he saw you leave by the west entrance." Forty Sideroad.

She nodded.

"You went down this trail here," I said, nodding at the one we had all followed up to the Lookout, "and when you reached the fork about a half a mile from here, you went west, right?"

She nodded.

"But that's not what Peter told you to do, was it?"

"He told me to be sure to take the long way around."

"Down the trail, around the lookout and out the south entrance, you mean?"

She nodded.

"Why didn't you?"

"I was mad at him. I'd had enough. He got a real kick out of telling me what to do. I couldn't stop him from blackmailing me, but I wasn't going to let him stage manage every detail of my life anymore."

"Just a little rebellion," I said, "but it sunk Thomas." I turned to him. "You came early to meet Peter that night, didn't you, Thomas? Were you planning right from the start to push him over the cliff? Were you going to hide and leap out at him?"

Nothing.

"But when you arrived early, you got a little surprise, didn't you? You saw Lise here and you found out she was being blackmailed too. And you heard Peter tell her to leave by the long way. That's why you told me that you saw her at the south entrance to the park. That's the exit you thought she used. But she didn't. She went out the west entrance. That's where the man saw her."

Thomas had been standing as still as a rock the whole time. I didn't know what he was thinking. Maybe he was trying to figure some way out. There wasn't one, though. Then, suddenly, he moved. Raced, really, right past me, heading for the trail. And then, just as suddenly, Matt was flying through the air. He tackled Thomas to the ground like a football linebacker.

Then the cavalry — well, the police — finally arrived. I'd been getting nervous that maybe Levesque hadn't found the note I'd pineappled to the fridge. He reached down and pulled Thomas to his feet. He did it as if he were a kindly passerby helping someone who had tripped and maybe hurt himself.

"I think you'd better come with me," he said.

# Chapter 17

It was late, after midnight, by the time Levesque finished his paperwork. He had suggested several times that I go home, but he never insisted on it. Finally, he got up from his desk, came over to where I was, and sat down beside me.

"Nice work," he said.

"Yeah." Yeah, not thanks.

"Problem?"

"I was going out with him."

I was seeing a guy who had let one guy drown and who had pushed another guy off a cliff. Sometimes a triumph can feel an awful lot like a defeat.

Levesque said nothing. Not, geez, tough break. Not, there's no way you could have known. Not even, time heals all wounds. He just sat there and waited. And, finally — Levesque works like raindrops on granite, he wears you down slowly, but he wears you down — it got to me and I asked.

"Did he tell you what happened?"

I wasn't really expecting an answer. I was prepared for the "official police investigation" routine. Instead I got, "On the lake or on MacAdam's Lookout?"

I stared at him. "You're actually going to tell me?"

He shrugged. "You figured out ninety-five percent of it yourself. I owe you the rest. But you're going to have to promise me to keep everything I tell you to yourself."

I nodded. Then I answered the question he had asked. "Both," I said. I wanted the whole story.

"He says what happened on the lake was an accident. He was out skating when Adam Gillette came along and challenged him to a race out to the marker. He accepted. He says he wasn't even thinking about ice conditions until he heard the sound."

"What sound?"

"The loud cracking sound lake ice makes when it's ready to let go. He heard it and knew right away what it was. He turned and started skating as fast as he could for shore. He says he assumed Adam was doing the same thing. It wasn't until he got far enough in to feel safe that he saw that Adam wasn't with him, that he had gone through the ice. He started back to try to help him, but there was another loud crack and he got scared."

"Scared he'd go through the ice himself?"

Levesque nodded.

"That's not what Peter said in his letter," I pointed out.

"No, it isn't. Peter's letter tells one story — the way things looked from where Peter was standing. Thomas tells another story. It's going to be up to the crown attorney, a couple of lawyers and maybe a judge and jury to figure out what really happened. I'm telling you what Thomas said, which is that he was too scared to move. He said he wanted to help Adam, but he was afraid to. He knew he should have at least gone for help, but he couldn't make up his mind to do that, either. He says he was pulled in two directions at once, until it was too late. Then he panicked and ran." He shook his head. "The funny thing is, Peter might never have known it was Thomas out there if Thomas hadn't given him a hard time a few days later."

My ears really pricked up now. In his letter, Peter had said that at first he didn't know who was on the ice. He hadn't been clear about exactly when he had identified the second person as Thomas.

"What happened?" I asked.

"Two days after Adam died, Thomas ran into Peter at school. He hassled Peter — I gather he did that a lot, jostled him, tried to unhook his backpack, teased him about knowing more about what was going on in space than what's going on in the real world. Apparently Peter got mad and said he knew plenty about the real world. He told Thomas he was on his way to the police station to tell them what he had seen the day Adam Gillette died. That's where Thomas got it all confused. He thought Peter knew it was him and was threatening him."

"But he wasn't?"

Levesque shook his head. "Thomas says he realized too late that Peter didn't actually know anything, until he saw Thomas's reaction. That seems to be when Peter put two and two together and realized who had been on the ice with Adam. Peter played the 9-1-1 tape for Thomas, to prove he'd been there when Adam drowned. Thomas offered him anything he wanted if he kept quiet. The way Thomas rationalized it, Adam was already dead — nothing anybody did would change that. But Thomas didn't want to be seen as a coward, or to be charged with anything. Apparently he didn't think his life should be ruined just because he panicked."

I wanted to believe it had been an accident. I wanted to believe anything except that Thomas was a cold-blooded murderer.

"What about what happened to Peter?" I asked.

"According to Thomas, that night in the park, Peter said he was going to the police. He said he couldn't keep the secret anymore."

I had to ask it. "Did Thomas push Peter off the lookout?"

"He says he tried to scare Peter into keeping quiet. He wanted to stop Peter from going to the authorities. He says Peter panicked and tried to get away. That's when he fell and went over the cliff."

"But what about the note then? There was that suicide note in Peter's pocket."

"Thomas put it there. After he went home, he got even more scared. He was afraid someone would think Peter had been pushed. So he typed up a note and went back into the park — "

"He went *back?* Wasn't he afraid he'd be seen?"

"He was still in a state of panic," Levesque said. "And he wanted to make sure it didn't even occur to anyone that Peter might have been pushed. So he went back and he stuffed the note into Peter's pocket. He admitted he even crumpled it up some so it would look like it had been in Peter's pocket before he jumped. You know, like it had been damaged in the fall, too."

Just thinking of that scenario made me shudder. Imagine reaching down, finding the pocket . . . "Do you believe him?" I asked Levesque.

"It's not my job to believe him."

A non-answer. I was in no mood for a non-answer. Thomas had said he wanted to stop Peter. Just how far had he gone to get that result?

"Do you believe Thomas?" I asked. "Do you believe that both deaths were accidents?"

Levesque sat quietly for a moment, looking at me, considering. Finally he said, "I don't know."

I couldn't see anything in his eyes or on his face that confirmed that, but I believed him. I didn't know, either, and that bothered me. But that wasn't the only thing bothering me.

"When I showed Thomas that letter, I told him it proved that Peter was going to turn him in," I said.

Silence. Then, "And?"

"And . . . that letter almost didn't get found." That was the other thing that was eating at me.

"But it did get found," Levesque said patiently. "You found it."

"Only because I was too lazy to get rid of all the

stuff Mrs. Flosnick gave me."

Levesque shook his head. He obviously didn't get it.

"That letter was sealed in an envelope addressed by Peter to himself," I said. "Peter Flosnick, *East Hastings Herald*, East Hastings Regional High School. That's what it said on the envelope. And it was in a whole pile of envelopes addressed the same way, envelopes that, after Peter's death, no one was ever going to open. If I hadn't been too lazy to get rid of them, they all would have been thrown out."

"So?"

"So if hiding the circumstances of Adam Gillette's death really got to be too hard for Peter, and if he really had been planning to turn Thomas in, why did he hide the letter where there was a good chance no one would ever find it?"

"Maybe he was more worried about making sure that Thomas wouldn't find it."

"Maybe," I said. But I wasn't positive I believed that. "Or maybe he liked the power he got from blackmailing people. Maybe he was just as bad as the rest of them." Didn't that make more sense? Fact: Peter had been shunned by kids who thought he was weird. Fact: He had taken his revenge through blackmail. Maybe he hadn't killed anyone, but that didn't exactly put him in the category of nice guy. Instead of coming forward with what he knew about Adam Gillette's death, he had used that information to get even. And he had hidden what he knew so well that it had been pure luck that I had stumbled across it. What did that say about *him*?

Levesque got up and lumbered over to his desk. He picked up a file folder, opened it, took something out of it, and came back to where I was.

"You see this?" he said, handing me a piece of paper. It was the first page of Peter's letter. Levesque was pointing at the date at the top of the letter.

"So?"

"So, this letter was written about five months after Adam Gillette's death, and more than six months after the fire at Clear Meadows."

I still didn't get it. "So?"

"So, maybe you're right about why Peter got involved in blackmail. Maybe it gave him power and maybe he liked that. But his last meeting with Thomas proves that he was having second thoughts."

"Then why did he hide the letter?"

"Maybe he got into a deeper hole than he bargained for," Levesque said. "Sometimes, when that happens, it's hard to climb back out."

"I don't understand — "

"By the time Peter wrote this letter, he had been blackmailing Thomas for five months. If you had been Thomas, and five months after he had been blackmailing you Peter threatened to tell what he knew, what would you have done?"

"I like to think that I wouldn't have panicked him

into falling over a cliff."

"I didn't ask what you wouldn't have done," Levesque said, but in a nice way, a gentle sort of way.

I thought for a few moments. Then, slowly, I said, "I probably would have said something like, if you show them yours, Peter, then I'll show them mine."

I had the impression that Levesque nodded just a little, but I wasn't positive.

"Meaning?" he said, drawing me out.

"Meaning, if I'd been Thomas, I would have admitted to Peter that not helping Adam was wrong." I thought I had it now. "But that using that kind of information to blackmail someone, instead of going to the police, was just as bad. Maybe even worse."

Now, for sure, Levesque was nodding.

"If Peter had told what he knew, after keeping quiet about it for so long, he would have come off looking as bad as Thomas," I said. It was really starting to make sense. "Maybe he'd look even worse. After all, he profited from Adam's death." I shook my head. "It would be kind of ironic if that's why he hid the letter."

"What do you mean?" Levesque said.

"Thomas says he didn't help Adam because he was too scared. If you're right, if Peter finally had a change of heart about what he had done and he didn't come forward because he was too scared, then he was just the same as Thomas, wasn't he?"

"But he was going to come forward," Levesque

said. "In the end, he found his courage and he confronted Thomas. It cost him his life. But because he wrote it down, and because you found his letter, everything has been brought to light."

"Everything?"

Levesque shrugged. "As much as possible, under the circumstances," he said. "Enough."

Maybe.

"You did good, Chloe," he said. "Only next time, don't wait so long before you tell me what's going on."

I looked over at his big, craggy face.

"Next time?" I said.